SCHOOLED IN MAGIC

Cordelia Cooper Book 2

Gorg Huff & Paula Goodlett

Cover designed by Laura Givens

Gorg Huff & Paula Goodlett
Visit my website at https://warspell.com/

Printed in the United States of America

First Printing: September 2021
1632, Inc.

eBook ISBN-13 : 978-1-956015-15-7
Trade Paperback ISBN-13 : 978-1-956015-16-4

CONTENTS

North →

Port Halcon

Orclands

Amourai

Elfsain

K.O.T.C.

Arginia

Skutes Wiles

Centraium

Kronisburg

Doichry

God Lands

Dragon Lands

Pango Island

Lizard Island

CHAPTER 1

Location: The Quad, University of Kronisburg
Date: 14 Banth, 772 AR (After Rime)

"That's fine, Cordelia. Now lock it in," Wizard Herlict said.

Cordelia locked it in. It was the last step in crafting the spell Adreana's Gossamer Wings, commonly known as the wings spell or just Wings. When invoked it would create a pair of ethereal wings. Since the wings weren't made of normal stuff but were actually made of magic, they passed through her clothing without tearing it, but they did push against the air because that was what they were designed to do.

"So, Cordelia, why did you use that particular variation in the third section?"

Cordelia blushed. She wasn't comfortable with her looks. About the only good feature she thought she had was long, straight black hair which did very much what she wanted it to. Still, getting any sort of fabrication past the Wizard Agnesse Herlict wasn't going to happen. "I, well, I wanted the feathers to match my hair," she got out in a rush.

"Perfectly reasonable choice," Wizard Herlict agreed with a grin. "One does want to look one's best when flying after all. Speaking of which, let's step out into the yard and test them out." The Yard was a green space in the university surrounded by five buildings and not all that visible to outsiders.

Cordelia had chosen this spell because it was among the most basic of spells that allowed you to fly. She was a skilled enough wizard to learn Coranith's Direct Flight, which allowed you to fly without wings, but Coranith's didn't last as long as Wings and required considerably more power to work. Now she was reconsidering that decision. She had known that she would have to learn to use the wings as well as create them. But now, as she followed Wizard Herlict out into the Yard, the prospect of learning to fly was becoming a great deal more daunting.

* * *

"All right, Cordelia. Invoke Wings and let's have a look at them."

Cordelia made a small gesture with her left hand accompanied by a mental image of complex shapes and colors, and a pair of translucent black wings suddenly appeared on her back. They went up almost five feet over her head before they folded and went back down to almost touch the ground. And she could feel them, sort of like her arms or legs. She felt the air as it caressed her wings. Even folded there was pressure on them and she felt their position. She knew they were folded because she could feel them.

Wizard Herlict nodded as she walked around Cordelia. "They seem well formed and of a good size. All right, now spread your wings."

Cordelia tried. Her left wing, where her mind happened to be focused, shot out like she was punching someone, but her right wing only opened about half way—in sympathy, the way your other fingers will copy part of the motion of a finger you try to curl. And now she could really feel the air. Even as light as the breeze was here in the Yard, surrounded by three- and four-story buildings, the breeze pushed against her wings in a noticeable way. She tried to stretch her right wing to match the position of her left, and it reached full extension, sliding through the air and pushing her to her left. She tried flapping and it worked all together too well. She was standing upright, and as her wings pushed forward her body was pushed backwards, and Cordelia landed on her rump.

"Well, that's the first thing almost everyone does, Wanderer Cooper. Birds, though they have only two legs, don't have an upright posture. They hold their bodies parallel to the ground, or at least not perpendicular to it. So when they flap the force is downward. If you stand upright and flap, the force is backwards. Let us try it again."

Cordelia wondered who "us" was, since she hardly thought Wizard Herlict's bottom was sore from landing on it. But she climbed back to her feet, or tried to.

Wings, as it happens, get in the way. They sprouted from her back, going from shoulder to waist. They were ethereal, so they didn't—for the most part—bang into things like the ground. But they did push against whatever they were moving through, and it was really hard to fold them when sitting down, and it was difficult to move with what amounted to sails attached to your back.

Herlict had had Cordelia craft an exceedingly weak version of Wings for her first try, so it only lasted fifteen minutes. Fully powered to the greatest level she could attain, it would last almost eight hours. But Cordelia didn't even manage the fifteen minutes. She dismissed her wings after ten minutes. Flying didn't appear to be something that came naturally to her. It did to some, she understood.

Wizard Herlict, for example, often flew for the sheer joy of it.

Location: Kronisburg
Date: 11 Zagrod, 772 AR (After Rime)

Cordelia Cooper ran down the street, her white wizard's robe with its silver and orange embroidery flapping around in the wind of her passage. *I really need to learn that flying spell, or practice more with Wings.* The reason she was running was because she was late to a lecture on spell research. It was one of her favorite subjects, in spite of the fact that she was a natural wizard. Cordelia rounded a corner and almost ran into a fruit-seller's cart. She skidded on the cobbles and flung up a hand, pushing against a wall that was ten feet away from her outflung hand and managed barely to avoid the cart.

"Sorry!" she shouted as she dashed past the cart and the surprised fruit seller. Actually, by now she was more Book Wizard than Natural, but she did have the natural affinity for magic and to a lot of wizards that talent defined her. A lot of the professors thought natural magic and magical research were like oil and water— things that didn't mix well. Unfortunately, Professor Sinjay was one of them. And being late would simply confirm his belief that Natural Wizards were flighty and undisciplined.

She had been talking to Bertie and Meggie at Das Vizart's Dank, and time had gotten away from her. The inn was owned by Meggie's family, and Cordelia rented a room there. Bertie was a fellow student and, well, good friends, good talk, and time slips away. She had passed her silver in book wizardry a month ago but was still only an orange in natural wizardry. Hence the interwoven orange and silver embroidery of her robes.

She whipped around another corner, deftly avoiding another accident and finally arrived at the lecture hall. She slipped through the door and stopped, as every head turned to look at her.

"Ah, Cordelia Cooper has deigned to join us," Professor Sinjay said, with a bit of a sneer. Cordelia thought it odd that Professor Sinjay thought so poorly of natural wizardry since he had studied magic at the University of Drakan, the most advanced college of wizardry in the world. "I realize that natural wizards think they can get by on talent alone. However, even a dragon's talent will not let you calculate the structure of a spell component."

Cordelia, with difficulty, refrained from entering into an argument with the professor. Professor Sinjay had a habit of baiting the natural wizards. Not that there were that many. The overwhelming majority of students at the wizard's college of the University of Kronisburg were Book Wizards. The most irritating thing was that, in a lot of ways, she agreed with him. She agreed that Book Wizardry was more flexible, and—in the long run— more powerful. That it led to a greater understanding of magic and how it worked. But Professor Sinjay always picked a point of disagreement. For understanding the structure of a spell component, the feel that a natural wizard had for the magic did help, though that feel wouldn't define the structure by itself. Wizard Sinjay didn't see it that way. He was trying to understand how magic worked. Trying, in fact, to turn magic into mathematical calculations. Which Cordelia thought was a great thing—if it could be done. She couldn't begin to follow the Topological Calculus he was working to develop as he tried to mathematically describe the internal structure of a spell. And she wasn't at all sure that it would yield up a better understanding than seeing magic since birth provided her. Cordelia generally had a feeling if a spell was going to do what she wanted. However, that feeling could be wrong and had been more than once. And she was all too aware of what could happen when feel wasn't enough. "Yes, sir. I'm sorry I'm late."

"Humph," Wizard Sinjay said, then went back to his lecture. "As I was saying, if you examine the component parts of the servant spell, you will see the purple coil has a slightly diminishing cross-section in its tube. This reflects the compressing of the magic and the complementary increase in intensity . . ."

And the lecture continued. It had been an amazing journey for Cordelia in the last two years. In some ways, university was more frightening than the time she had spent in the Patty Orc caves. Granted, no one—no one at the college itself—had tried to sacrifice her. At least not physically. She sometimes felt that her brain was going to explode from all the knowledge they were trying to shove into it. Or that she might kill herself by making a mistake and botching a spell.

Yet she loved this. The professors, the other students, talking in the market place about how this spell was crafted and how it might be modified to do this or that thing. And trying to understand why this structure of magic did something and another structure, almost the same, did nothing at all. Or at least nothing that she was aware of. Some of the professors insisted that every spell did something; that every magical structure, even those created by an utterly unaware person thinking about fish then frogs, had some effect on the real world in some way.

Cordelia pulled her mind back to the subject and listened to the lecture, trying to follow the wizard's math.

✱ ✱ ✱

Her next class was History of Centraium, in which she learned about the great Dwarven Empire that had ruled the world—or at least most of the continent of Centraium—from 1500 to 800 years ago. This class had helped her understand the reason behind the dwarven town she and her friends had explored last summer. And in a larger sense, it had helped her understand how governments and empires worked. For the modern nations of Centraium and Amonrai were very much the heirs of the

Dwarven Empire. The basic structure of their laws and government came from the dwarves. And that was the other thing that she loved about the university here at Kronisburg. For she was not only learning magic, she was learning history and philosophy. She was learning about the gods, and the people who followed them. She could almost feel herself growing.

* * *

"What caused the collapse of the Dwarven Empire?" Bertie asked. Rather portentously, Cordelia thought.

"Tell us, O sage, what caused the collapse?" Heinric Gotern asked.

"The weather," Bertie proclaimed.

"Ah, Bertie," Meggie pointed out. "The dwarves build underground."

"Ah, yourself," Bertie said. "Plants don't grow underground. Professor Horstein insists that the cooling that took place from 653 DE to 715 DE produced a lack of agricultural products, which started the revolts and worsened the inter-clan rivalries to the extent that the dwarves were unable to keep the humans under control."

"I thought it was because the gods got angry with the dwarves and encouraged the humans to revolt?" Cordelia asked. That was the common theory she had learned first in the little village she came from.

"Well, that may be the final cause," Bertie said, "but it just begs the question: why did the gods get so annoyed with the dwarves as to set dwarven clan against dwarven clan and bring down their empire?"

"So why did they?" Meggie asked. They were all having a beer in her father's inn. While Bertie was still a student of wizardry, he had, since the return from the caverns of Hoctbatch County, focused on a more rounded education and had used most of the wealth he had gained to buy into the inn. He still had his title but was fitting himself into the role of prosperous burgher quite well.

"They got mad at the way the dwarves were treating humans, and the other races, for that matter. And according to Professor Horstein, the dwarves were treating us badly because the weather put a crimp in the production of little things like food. And when there wasn't enough to go around, the humans got to starve. Which caused them to complain to the gods. But Noron was just a sport god at the time, mostly worshiped by those entering the arena."

"That's not true!" Juana Espino said with some heat. Juana was in the college of medicine, mostly because she had been told that she didn't have the right mindset for the college of theology. She was a thoroughgoing adherent of Noron, as was her whole family, and to hear her tell it, the whole nation of Nasine. "Noron was a great god even in the time of the Dwarven Empire. He just wasn't recognized as such."

"Theological debates," Meggie said, giving Bertie a hard look, "belong in the college of theology. Bertie shouldn't have brought it up."

"Sorry, love, but it was part and parcel of the prof's argument. The tensions in the Dwarven Empire are what gave the human gods an opening to become the major pantheon."

"They were always . . ."

"Ah hum!" Meggie interrupted.

"Yes, I know. But this notion that the gods change, that they get stronger or weaker, is sacrilegious. Noron is the god of honor and valor, the noblest of the gods and the judge of princes. He always has been and always will be. It is only human lack of understanding that has hidden that from the world," Juana insisted with considerable belligerence.

Cordelia held her peace. The religion of the Nasine Empire was polytheistic, but only sort of. They were devoted to Noron, not Timu, who was generally considered the father of the human gods. The dwarves had their own version of Timu, who they called Grugan. Barra, the human goddess of the harvest, was generally considered to be Timu's spouse and the mother of the gods. Except, of course, in those instances when Timu strayed. Which he apparently did with some regularity. However, Barra was not totally devoted to Timu, either. Cordelia thought it must be an interesting family life. For instance, Zagrod, the god of knowledge and book wizardry, was the child of Barra and a human scholar. Barra had been a Dwarven Goddess not married to Grugan during the Dwarven Empire, but after she became human she married Timu, though she continued having the occasional relationship with other gods, dragons and even mortals. Barra always had a soft place in her heart for humans because they tilled the earth and apparently Barra liked being tilled.

That is, all this was true assuming that the Intercessors were correct in their assumptions. The gods themselves were rather reticent about their relationships to one another.

The conversation went on, and as it moved away from the gods, Juana became less tense. In most ways, Juana was a perfectly decent young woman, but her religious certainty could be a bit wearing.

Meanwhile, Cordelia was feeling the effects of a long day and decided to retreat to her room and get some sleep.

Location: Das Vizart's Dank, Kronisburg
Date: 17 Wovoro, 772 AR

Cordelia sat in her room and looked at the letter in concern. She was rarely anywhere near the university's chancellery, so didn't often stop in. She hadn't heard from her family, although she had sent a letter two years ago, when she got to Kronisburg. In all that time, there had been no response. She hadn't really expected it. Mail was slow, having to be transported by whatever ship might be headed for the continent of its destination. Besides, no one in her family could read and she was unsure how quickly the village intercessor would get around to reading her letter to them.

So she was surprised to get a note at her room telling her that she needed to stop by the chancellery and pick up some mail. She wondered why the mail hadn't been forwarded to her rooms instead of her being required to go pick it up, but rules were like that. They didn't always make sense.

The next day, Cordelia stopped at the chancellery and picked up a letter. It was from the village of Greenshire, her home. So here she was, with letter in hand. She opened it and began to read.

To Cordelia Cooper, Apprentice Wizard

It is not the place of us in this small village to deal with wizardry or those who deal in it. The true and proper magic of the world is the Magic of Barra and the other good gods. Wizardry is not for us. While your family wishes you well for the blood you share, your presence is not welcome. We must look to the welfare of our souls when we enter the Halls of Coganie, Keeper of Souls.

Your family is doing well enough, in spite of the cost of your apprenticeship, although your father is failing. Your brother Michael has taken over the farm and recently married. There is a child on the way. A marriage is being arranged for your sister, Susan, although it will not take place for several years. Elenora and Robbie do well.

I take it upon myself to ask that, if possible, you provide some small return of your family's investment in your training. The money they spent to buy you your future and secure the village from your influence has not been recovered in the ensuing years. Rather the reverse, in fact. Needed tools couldn't be replaced till the old had broken and failed. The family and village are weakened by the loss of income.

Signed,

Torson, Intercessor of Barra

Cordelia read the letter, then read it again. Then she crumpled it in her fist, threw it against the wall and stomped around her room for a while. Crying and hurt, angry beyond measure, she raged at Torson, her father, and her brother.

Then she stopped.

True, Torson was an intercessor of Barra, but he was ignorant. He'd always been ignorant. Provincial, stuck in Greenshire, not wanting more. A fool.

No one in her family could read or write. They might not know what Torson had written. Probably didn't know.

She remembered Michael, and how worried he was when she was forced to leave with Rojer Cartwright, her so-called master and teacher—who didn't teach all that well. Who had tried to keep her illiterate. Probably from fear.

Fear.

That was what motivated Torson. He wasn't like the professors and intercessors in Centraium, and especially not like those here at the university.

It was hard to remember what life had been like in the village, what people had believed and felt: "Wizards were dangerous creatures who practiced horrid rites, sacrificed animals and even people to gain their magic." Untrained wizardry was even worse. It hadn't been an issue till that last year at home, but in that time she had realized that she terrified them all. Since then, dealing with the Kingdom Orcland Trading Company and the university, she had forgotten how normal people felt about wizards.

Well, all right then. If her family needed help, she would send help.

But she would do it her way.

* * *

Cordelia packed up a box for her family. In it, she included a bit of coin, although not much of that. Centraium coins weren't common in Amonrai, anyway. Mostly she packed amulets of cleaning. She had several that were permanent amulets. They should be saleable for a reasonable sum of money. It should be enough to put her family back on its feet and if they didn't want her to endanger their souls with her wizardry, well, there were other places in the world. Places where she was welcome, or at least not shunned.

The package had five of the cleaning amulets that she had made since she had gotten to the college. Unlike the little whisk brooms that Rojer had had her make as an apprentice, these were carefully designed to fit and reinforce the spell. Rojer hadn't really known that much about the making of magical items.

CHAPTER 2

Location: Classroom, University of Kronisburg
Date: 17 Barra, 772 AR

Back in classes, Law this time, the legal differences between the Kingdom Isles and Doichry, where Kronisburg was located. "Doichry has a more dwarven law system because the Empire only ever reached one of the four main Kingdom Islands," Professor Dolin said. Dolin was the Dwarvish word for "strong arms." Professor Dolin, in fact, didn't have particularly strong arms, at least not for a dwarf. A fact he had pointed out on the first day of class. "I teach here," he had told them, "because it's the only place I can go where my family name is not a lie." Then he'd laughed, sounding like grinding rocks, and continued, "Besides, I don't find humans as revolting as most of my fellows do."

Dwarves as a group didn't care much for the other races, considering only dragons to be their social equals, and all the other races as lesser races. Humans were the least hated of the other races, but even humans were considered to be nothing more than jumped-up slaves. Honestly, Professor Dolin wasn't like most dwarves in that respect. He treated all his students pretty much the same and Cordelia had seen nothing of real prejudice in him, though he loved to make jokes about it.

"The Kingdom laws came mostly out of their traditions, with the Empire's main effect being to codify the laws they already had."

"Is their law more primitive then?" asked a student.

"That's a somewhat prejudicial way of putting it," Professor Dolin said. "Kingdom commercial law has imported quite a bit of dwarven law, but their criminal law is in many ways superior to dwarven custom, focusing as it does more on individual responsibility and less on clan responsibility. For instance, the Dwarven Empire never developed the Kingdom's Charter of Human Rights. A charter that in the Kingdom itself, anyway, has now been extended to the other races."

"Or so they claim," Miguel Cordoba pronounced. "They don't follow their own laws in the Orclands, and Amonrai has actual chattel slavery of elves, at least in the southern provinces."

Cordelia kept her mouth shut. Miguel was a theology student and Junior Intercessor of Noron. He was also a young man who despised the Kingdom, and Amonrai even more than the Kingdom itself. The trade wars between the Nasine Empire and the Kingdom Isles had become real fighting wars several times over the last century and a lot of people on both sides thought of the other side as their natural enemy. Doichry had had considerable input into the formation of the Amonrai kingdom, but Nasine had been frozen out of the entire continent of Amonrai. There were a few Nasine colonists in Amonrai, but the nobility only included those from Doichry and the Kingdom Isles.

* * *

Cordelia got back to *Das Vizart's Dank* and found yet another note from the Chancellery. Still wondering just why they hadn't sent the letter to her lodgings instead of a note, she shook her head and headed for the Chancellery.

Cordelia showed the clerk the note. "A letter for me?" she asked.

The clerk smiled. "Yes, dear. Just let me get it for you."

No one had called Cordelia "dear" in years. But the middle-aged clerk was a nice woman, so she just smiled in response. "Thank you."

The clerk soon delivered the letter and Cordelia took it back to her lodgings to read it in privacy. If it was from her family again, she didn't want to be in anyone's view when she read it.

It wasn't from her family. There had been three letters over the last two years about the prize money from the smuggler she, the sea elves and the lizardmen had taken into custody on Pango Island. This one informed her that the case had been settled, and that all of the funds awarded had gone either to the legal fees or to the fees paid her factor for handling the matter. No accounting of what was spent on what was included. Cordelia wasn't able to interpret the legalese so she decided to take it over to the college of law.

Location: College of Law, University of Kronisburg
Date: 18 Barra, 772 AR

"Who can interpret a letter from a lawyer for me?" she asked the lad at the desk. He looked to be perhaps fourteen, with a curl of blond hair falling down the center of his forehead and a curly blond cowlick in back.

He grinned. "A demon or other infernal power might manage it."

Cordelia laughed. "Do you happen to know anyone with infernal powers?"

"I'm afraid not," he said. "They're all afraid of coming to the college of law."

"Well, then . . . perhaps a law student?"

"You'd be safer with an infernal power, but all right. I'll have a look."

"Um . . . no offense," Cordelia said, eyeing his youth. "But what year are you?"

"Third, actually." He grinned again. "Looking younger is my abiding curse. No one sees the evil that lurks inside. Bwahahahahah!"

Laughing, Cordelia handed over the letter.

He read it over and his smile died. He looked at her and suddenly looked a great deal more serious and at least two years older. "You were involved in the taking of a pirate off the island of Pango?" he asked.

"Well, it was actually a smuggler, but yes," Cordelia said.

"And you were in command?"

"Pretty much, yes."

"This is essentially a letter to inform you that you have been . . . ah . . . cut out of the loot, as it were. All the monies that the prize court eventually granted were divided between the lawyers and your factor. Was there someone you left to manage the affair for you when you came here?"

"Yes. Mrs. Amelia Tomson. The smuggler was coming into the little bay where they lived when we took it. It was me, a bunch of sea elves and some lizardmen. Her husband was deeply involved with the smugglers and there were enough questions that the governor of the island, Andrew Hopkins, delayed things until I had to leave. I would have put the whole matter in the charge of the sea elves, but, unfortunately, the regulations of the Kingdom Orcland Trading Company, at least as they're interpreted on Pango, effectively prohibit that.

"Did the sea elves and the lizardmen at least get their share?"

"I doubt it," he said. "The way this reads is strongly suggestive that you stay away from Pango Island for the rest of your life. Because, according to this, not only was all the prize money used up, you are considerably in debt to the factor you appointed."

Cordelia just looked at him. Honestly, by the end of last year she hadn't expected to ever see anything of the prize money. But this . . . this was too much. She didn't mind losing the money and she didn't need it, really. But to be warned off that ragged little island, and told she was in debt to enforce that edict? That was outrageous. More importantly, she had promised the sea elves and the lizardmen that they would get their share. That they would be freed. And now it looked like they weren't. She couldn't be absolutely sure of that, not from Doichry. But it didn't look good. And now she was forsworn, as far as she knew.

"Thank you," Cordelia said, retrieving her letter. "I'm going to have to think about this."

* * *

Professor Dolin looked at the letter the next day and confirmed what the law student had said. He even identified the student. "Master Harris is from the Kingdom Isles and one of our brighter third-year students. Don't let his innocent airs fool you, as they have so many of the young ladies studying here at the university. His analysis of your situation is entirely accurate; this is an excellent example of the misuse of legal technicalities and why you should never leave a factor with too much authority, even one you have every reason to think you can trust. With your permission, Wanderer Cooper, I would like to use this letter in class today. Especially those of you who are not going into the law need to realize that these things matter."

So, with Cordelia's permission, Professor Dolin rearranged the class schedule a bit and spent the day discussing contracts, factors, and the dangers of leaving people with too much authority.

17

"In this case," he continued, "Wanderer Cooper failed to set the wage that Mrs. Tomson was to be paid and thereby allowed Mrs. Tomson to set her own wage, which was set at such a level that by the time the prize had been awarded, it and more was owed to her for managing the affair. Clearly, Wanderer Cooper thought she had every reason to trust Mrs. Tomson, or she would not have given her such power."

"That's the problem with Kingdom law. And especially the laws of the KOTC. It's ridiculous having a company setting its own law," Miguel Cordoba said. "There is no recourse to honor. It is an offense against Noron and all persons of integrity."

"Ah, but, Senor Cordoba," Professor Dolin said, "the Nasine legal system is no more secure. Yes, the better swordsman wins, but the better swordsman is not necessarily in the right."

"The person in the right is going to win the duel," Miguel said. "Because Noron will see to it."

At which point Professor Dolin went through a list of prominent duels that had later been shown to have been won by the person who was not, in fact, in the right. He even brought up the issue of paid duelists, which left poor Miguel red-faced and furious, but without an answer.

Location: Das Vizart's Dank, Kronisburg
Date: 24 Barra, 772 AR

"Well, Cordelia," Miguel said after taking a sip of *Das Vizart's Dank*'s very good beer. "I have given the professor's words much thought. And I have come to the conclusion that it is the duty of men of honor to take up the cause in such cases as yours. For, when legal trickery, or even paid duelists, bring about an unjust result the only true solution is for men of honor to correct the faulty system," he said very portentously.

"Is that what Noron tells you?" Cordelia asked.

"Not in so many words," Miguel admitted. "But while I was praying on the matter, I received a spell to heal wounds. I cannot be sure, for as it happened, the spell was very useful later that day. But I believe that Noron was expressing his approval of my conclusion."

"Noron gives you spells?" Cordelia asked, shocked and sounding like it. She wouldn't have guessed that Miguel would be the sort to get spells. Not that she had ever known an intercessor who received spells. She had thought you had to be sort of holy or something like that and Cordoba was a stubborn horse's hind end most of the time.

Miguel Cordoba actually grinned, "I must admit this was the first time. Which is another reason that I am convinced that I must accompany you on your quest to restore your rightful gains, in spite of the fact that you earned it by seizing a Nasine ship. For I must grant that the ship was involved in illegal activities."

"First, I haven't even decided that I will embark on any such quest. Second, if I did, it would be to see to it that the sea elves and the lizardmen were being treated fairly. And third, I don't recall inviting you."

"But—" Miguel stopped, clearly making himself think about what she had said. Then he continued, "Again I am instructed. This then is what makes it such a worthy quest. You embark not for your own glory or, worse, your own wealth, however honorably earned. Instead, your quest is centered on the welfare of your loyal liegemen. Of course you will go on the quest. It is your clear duty. As to your not inviting me . . . how could you when you hadn't confirmed in your own mind that you would take up the gauntlet? In Noron's good time, you will invite me along."

Meggie started laughing so hard that she nearly dropped the beer pitcher. Bertie grinned and said, "Well, you know, Cordelia, an intercessor with healing spells is always useful on an adventure."

"But I don't want to go on an adventure. I just made silver a couple of months ago."

"And what about the lizardmen?" Meggie asked.

Cordelia set her beer down with a thump.

"And the sea elves," Bertie pointed out. "From what you told us, they risked a lot to take that ship. And you're the one who talked them into it."

"That's not fair," Cordelia said, and then almost threw her beer at Miguel when she saw him grinning.

What made it all worse was that her friends were right. The sea elves and the lizardmen had risked a great deal to help her, based on her promise that they would gain a better life. And that is what she had assumed had happened. If that wasn't what happened, she owed them.

One thing that Cordelia wasn't, was particularly devoted to the gods. Most people had no personal experience with the gods, only knowing them through their intercessors. And most intercessors were working secondhand since only a small percentage of the intercessors actually received spells. Even those were rarely actually spoken to by gods because the human mind couldn't handle it. So the gods gave signs and portents. The re-sanctification of the temple in the dwarven caverns to Justain, God of Law, had been a special case made possible by Lord Karl's sacrifice.

Actually, Cordelia had a lot more experience with the gods than most people, but those personal experiences weren't the sort to inspire devotion. For instance, Koteck, the god of the Patty Orcs, liked to torture her victims to death. Balrak, the dwarven god who had created the lich in the caverns, also required sacrifice. Even the so-called good god of Justice, Justain, only actually talked to the guard captain after getting a human sacrifice dedicated to him. So having an Intercessor along who was in regular contact with a god, especially Noron—who, while not exactly evil, was not exactly a favorite of the Kingdom or Amonrai . . . the whole trial-by-combat thing struck Cordelia as more than a little barbaric.

Location: Sanctum of Noron, College of Theology, University of Kronisburg
Date: 26 Barra, 772 AR

As it happened, even while Cordelia was thinking such thoughts, Miguel was hearing the other side of the argument from his teachers. The University of Kronisburg was naturally dedicated to Zagrod, the god of knowledge. But its faculty included intercessors of all the major gods. There were a number of intercessors of Noron, and most of them were from the Nasine Empire, or were at least its partisans.

High Intercessor Alvarez looked down his pointed nose at Miguel. "Young man, surely you can see that the notion of going off on a quest to restore the fortunes of a young natural wizard adventurer, especially *that* one, who is little more than a pirate herself, is unlikely to be what Noron wants."

"Yes, I can, High Intercessor," Miguel said. "In fact, as I started my prayers the day before yesterday, that was exactly my view of the situation. What I prayed to Noron for was the means to persuade Professor Dorgin and Cordelia herself of the error of their conclusions. But the more I prayed over and thought about the matter, the more I was forced, much against my will, Intercessor, to the conclusion that Cordelia's actions were, in fact, justified under the law of that island."

"The laws of a company? Not a nation? No law at all. Simply the promulgations of a bunch of plutocrats." High Intercessor Alvarez sniffed.

"Again, I agree, High Intercessor," Miguel said. "But Cordelia was an employee of that company. Surely she was bound by its regulations?"

"Possibly. But that does not justify her actions."

"With respect, High Intercessor, by the law of Noron and the law of honor, it does. And it was when I had reached that conclusion, that I felt Noron's touch, and was gifted with spells."

"I can't say I approve of your conclusions," Alvarez said. "And I find it especially disturbing in your case, for it is rare that one is given the honor of the god's touch. I have served Noron these past thirty years and I do not receive spells. So I cannot order you not to go. But I strongly recommend that you reconsider. Nor will the temple in any way fund this madness."

That was a real shame, for although Miguel was of gentry blood, his family owned little property and he was seldom in funds.

✳ ✳ ✳

"So I have to pay your way," Cordelia said. "If I take you."

"Well, you must ask the gods what you should do," Miguel said.

"I don't recall the gods having done me that many favors," Cordelia pointed out.

Miguel, looking shocked, said, "But the gods are the gods."

"And the dragons are dragons," Cordelia said. "Which means I need to be careful of them, but doesn't mean I want to go traipsing into their caves. I am perfectly happy to leave the gods to their godly endeavors, if they will leave me to mine."

Miguel was looking even more shocked, but after a moment of outraged indignation he calmed down. "The gods control the allocation of your soul, Cordelia. Having a dragon mad at you is much safer and a much more temporary concern. Listen to me, please. Those orcs who were tortured by Koteck's priestess are still being tortured by Koteck. The boy who was killed by Balrak and all his other victims would still be in his clutches if not for the intercession of Justain. We humans don't always understand what they want but it is unwise to ignore their will."

"Sounds like the gods are a good bunch to stay away from then."

"Perhaps. If you could. But soon or late you will come to Coganie's hall and face the judgment of Justain. When that day comes, not having acts in support of and contrition to the gods will leave you in poor stead."

"So it's all just about fear, then? Do what the gods want or suffer the consequences, no matter whether it's right or wrong?"

"No, not entirely. That is why there is more than one god. We are unsure what is right and what is right for our natures. Not everyone feels the same right, or is drawn to the same god. Some go where their interest lies, to the god that offers them the most. They are the ones who follow the evil gods. But some of us go where our honor or compassion lead us. We follow the good gods."

"But why should we follow at all? Why not go our own way?"

"You can try that," Miguel said, smiling. "But that doesn't mean you will succeed. Nor does it mean that it's *your* own way. It could very well be the way a god has sent you."

Location: University Pantheon, University of Kronisberg
Date: 29 Barra, 772 AR

Much against her will, Cordelia was in the university pantheon, a large temple dedicated to the main gods of Centraium. She had been talked into it as much by Meggie and Bertie as by Miguel. Bertie had even suggested that she might talk Miguel out of going by offending Noron.

So she was looking at the alcoves around the large, circular building. Each god had its own alcove. There were representations of Zagrod, the only god she felt much affinity for, but also Noron, Justain, Barra, Dugon and others, mostly in their human forms—except for Dugon—because this was a human temple. The whole pantheon was awash in subtle magic. So subtle was this magic that it was almost hard to tell from the regular background of magic that she felt anywhere. But it *was* different magic, formed by the interwoven spells of gods, granted to their intercessors over the centuries.

It was terrifying.

Not just the power, but the subtlety, the way the spells interwove, canceling and reinforcing one another as the gods played whatever precedence games they played. For a natural wizard, there were two buildings here, the one built by men and the one built by the gods themselves through the effects of their spells. There were intercessors everywhere, as well as petitioners, mostly in their best clothing. Asking the gods for help, or promising the gods gifts, if only the gods would let them gain this or that advantage. And Cordelia couldn't help wondering why the gods cared. What could a mere human give a being that could create the spells she saw?

There were sacrifices being made that reminded her of the Patty Orc caves. They weren't human, in fact they were mostly rabbits and the like, though there were a number of pigs and some cattle. Somehow the pigs bothered her most, because her family had had pigs on the farm and pigs are pretty smart animals. It had never bothered her when they had butchered a pig for the table, in spite of the fact that the colors around a pig were stronger than those around a cow, even though the cow was bigger. She had seen sacrifices in the village temple when she was a little girl. The same thing happened here as there. The colors seemed to be sucked away into the altar, just like they had at the Patty Orc's cave.

Cordelia settled on a bench in front of Zagrod's altar, thinking. As much as she didn't really want to make a trip to Pango Island, she did have a responsibility to the sea elves and the lizardmen. She sighed. So be it. Even if it cost all the money she had put aside for the next two years of school, she had to go to Pango.

Location: Das Vizards Dank
Date: 29 Barra, 772 AR

Cordelia was going through her books and a listing of spells available to her from the school's collection. Available to her, but not for free. She looked over at her applied magic instructor. "What do you think?"

Master Wizard Gorick took a swig of the good dark beer they made here and set the mug on the table. "Well, Journeywoman Cooper, if you're determined to go off on this silly quest of yours, the first thing we look at is your spells, the ones you already have in your spell book."

Cordelia pulled out her books. Both her own, mostly constructed in the two years that she'd been at university, and also the spell book she had recovered from the elven stronghold in Amonrai. She had the skill to craft all of hers, but only a few of those in the one from Amonrai.

Master Wizard Gorick looked at her spells. "Well, it's a decent collection. I wish you had a few more defensive spells, Armored Robes or Wizard Cloak. Even Wizard Shield can be useful. Do you have Wizard Bolt internalized?"

"Yes, ma'am."

"Good, make sure you use it enough to keep it internalized, even if it means shooting at nothing at all."

"I do, ma'am. I use it once a day, every day."

"In that case, you want Armored Robes. You have the credits to buy that one left over from the sale of Grease Axle to the school. You seem to be well stocked with the work-a-day spells. That's good. You would be surprised at how many of the young adventuring wizards forget those and end up spending half their treasure having people darn their socks or repair their horse's harness. You have Wings. You want to practice that, and you need to work on Lighten Me. Sometimes you don't want to be flying around in sight of who knows what. And a wizard wearing wings in the Dragon Lands is like a sparrow in a hawk's hunting ground. So work on that one."

Gorick set the book aside and had a bite of the smoked sausage and sauerkraut, carefully wiped her hands, then went back to the book. It was a smooth and well-practiced routine. Automatic protection of spell books from messes was a part of a wizard's training and so conditioned into wizards that they can't pick up a week old newspaper without wiping their hands first.

"Pick Locks? No, I don't think so. For one thing, you're a natural and even if you learned it, you would still have to craft it to each particular lock. You're better off just using your natural magic sense to see the locking mechanism and shift it by Wizard's Will."

Wizard's Will was Gorik's way of referring to the ability of a natural wizard to manipulate magic directly to do things like produce light, see through walls if they weren't too thick or, as in this case, turn the tumblers in a lock.

"Hm. You ought to get rid of this ageing spell. It's unhealthy." Gorik held up a hand. "None of my business, Cordelia. Just my opinion.

"You have Lighten Stuff internalized. Why is that?"

"My bag of holding doesn't affect weight."

"Hmm, makes sense, I guess. I don't recommend Draw Water. It works fine if there is a lot of humidity in the air, but in a dry climate, not so well. Of course, you're heading for a tropical island, so it ought to work there, and it is a lot easier than Create Water. But everywhere on your trip isn't going to be the tropics. And Purify Water works on salt water, so it will work in any climate. I would recommend that instead of Draw Water.

Shape Stone is useful in making stuff, but I don't see it as being of much use on a trip like this.

"That, and I know you've been making servant amulets since you got to school." Garik nodded. "I think this is all you can afford."

Cordelia agreed. She was out of credits with the Magic Department, and fairly short on cash.

CHAPTER 3

Location: Sanctum of Zagrod, College of Theology,
University of Kronisburg
Date: 30 Barra, 772 AR

"Well, sir," Cordelia said to High Intercessor Sawnell, "it's because I have to go. In all honesty, I don't really want to leave school at this time. I wanted . . ." She paused and looked out the window at the university where she'd been so busy and happy. ". . . I wanted to finish my studies. And I will!" Cordelia added fiercely. "Somehow I'll come back and learn enough to wear the purple of a full wizard." Then she sighed. "But they risked their lives on my say-so, and if they aren't getting what's due them, I have to fix it."

High Intercessor Sawnell was as close to a mentor as Cordelia had, due to his relationship with the Brooks family she had met in the Orclands. He nodded at her explanation. "I understand, Cordelia, indeed I do. But High Intercessor Alvarez is having fits and asked for this meeting."

"It wasn't my idea for Miguel to go along," Cordelia said. "If High Intercessor Alvarez can talk him out of it, that's fine with me. He says that receiving spells after he decided that he should go along means that Noron approves but I'm not sure I believe that. The truth is, I don't really understand signs and portents."

"I'm not sure anyone really does," High Intercessor Sawnell admitted, while leading her down the hall. "It's a bit like walking a ridge pole on a tall building, high in the air. When things work out right, you're safe. But one small slip and you can face a heck of a fall. Meanwhile, let's just go see them and perhaps things can be worked out."

"I suppose." Cordelia's face creased in concern. "When I go, it would be good to have Miguel. I'll probably need him. Someone will get hurt, because someone always does. An intercessor with healing spells might keep someone from dying."

"Part of it is simply that Miguel is quite young and it's even rarer for intercessors to receive spells that young. That makes him valuable."

They turned a corner and walked through a door to a cosy room with a table and a half-dozen comfortable chairs. Miguel and an older, sharp-faced man with dark hair and a black goatee and mustache waited for them.

"Welcome, High Intercessor Sawnell," he said with a pronounced Nasine accent. He looked Cordelia up and down like she was getting ready to steal his innocent child for sacrifice.

"Hello, Ramon," High Intercessor Sawnell said. "Go ahead and have a seat, Cordelia. This isn't formal."

Cordelia guessed by High Intercessor Alvarez's expression that he would have much preferred to keep things formal. But Intercessor Sawnell wasn't having it. She grinned and took a seat.

"The question at issue is whether Miguel has received a true sign or been distracted by a pretty face," Ramon Alvarez said. He looked over at Cordelia and seemed to reconsider.

Which actually didn't come as much of a shock to Cordelia. She was a bit on the short and stocky side, with black hair and a round face. Her face could be pleasant enough, but it would never launch a thousand ships. Not even a raft.

"Or the chance for glory," Alvarez corrected.

"His chastity is safe with me," Cordelia said and Miguel blushed. "For that matter, it wasn't my idea to have him along, though I will admit that if trouble happens, having an intercessor's healing spells handy wouldn't hurt. I don't know if he'd be any good in a fight, though."

"I am of the Nasine gentry," Miguel said, sounding offended. "We learn to use the sword before we learn to walk!"

"Overconfidence is not going to help you," Cordelia pointed out. "A black lion can get past a sword, Miguel. I've seen it happen. And a skeleton doesn't care if you stab him in the chest, since it doesn't have flesh or blood."

Intercessor Alvarez was smiling, apparently in the hope that Cordelia would persuade Miguel that he didn't want to go after all. His hopes, however, were soon dashed.

"Noron wishes me to accompany you," Miguel said. "I will be careful."

Intercessor Alvarez's face fell. "It is not a true sign," he insisted.

"How do you know?" asked High Intercessor Sawnell.

"Because it cannot be! He's only seventeen!"

"He's old enough to receive the spells," Sawnell pointed out. "And you know as well as I do that we're guessing about what is and isn't a sign."

"We're not guessing," Alvarez said. "We're hearing the gods whisper to us!"

"If Noron ever actually whispered to you, Ramon, it would turn you into a dribbling idiot. You have to be as stubborn as a mule to deal with a god."

"Now it makes sense," Cordelia said.

And High Intercessor Sawnell laughed out loud. "What those who don't have the experience of being touched by a god don't understand is that it takes a very strong will to come through the experience whole. I was putting it poorly when I said you have to be stubborn as a mule. But not that poorly. It takes a very strong sense of self and most children, in spite of how stubborn they sometimes seem, don't have that strong a sense of self. Hard and brittle, not strong. That's why it's so rare that even young adults are touched by the gods."

"What about the Intercessors of Koteck?" Cordelia asked. "Honestly, they didn't strike me as . . . having that strong a character?"

"Two things, I think, probably explain the matter. First, they were probably quite insane by the time you met them. Dealing directly with gods doesn't turn everyone catatonic. Many simply lose all sense of empathy, all awareness of anyone else's feelings, because the god and the god's will become all that matters. So the priestess didn't see you or the orcs that she sacrificed to Koteck as people at all, just things that her god wanted. The second thing is that the sacrifices themselves took the brunt of Koteck's contact. And most of the magic was delivered in the creation of magical items so the priestess was less affected. As to the lich, it was, by the time you met it, little more than a toy to its god, having very little will left to do anything but what Balrak wanted."

Cordelia nodded and Intercessor Alvarez was looking at her in apparent surprise. "You're the one who went to old Hoctbatch?"

"One of them," Cordelia acknowledged.

"Well, sanctifying the place to Justain was well enough done, I admit, though the whole adventure was poorly planned."

Cordelia held her peace. Intercessor Alvarez was right in a way. There were a number of things that, in hindsight, should have been done differently. But Cordelia was coming to believe that there were always things that should have been done differently in hindsight. She almost pointed that out, but decided that it wouldn't make any difference.

"In fact, you seem inclined toward poorly planned adventures. The taking of the *Conquistador* was hardly well thought out."

"Actually, sir, the taking of the ship was quite well thought out and accomplished with very little in the way of casualties on either side,"

Cordelia said "Even Mr. Tomson died only because he attacked me in a situation where even had he succeeded he would have gained little by it."

"Then why do you feel the need to go back?" he looked down his nose at her.

"Because after she left, things wandered away from the path she had set them on. Which can hardly be laid at Cordelia's feet." High Intercessor Sawnell came to Cordelia's rescue.

It was becoming fairly clear to Cordelia that High Intercessor Alvarez hadn't brought her here for a talk but for an inquisition. Something that the intercessors of Noron in the Nasine Empire were becoming known for. Well, if she was to be put to the question she had some of her own to put.

"High Intercessor Alvarez, why is it that the gods don't just tone it down a bit so that they can talk to ordinary mortals? Is it that they just don't care about ordinary people enough to limit their voices to something we can deal with?" It wasn't a question that she had ever put to High Intercessor Sawnell because it was the sort of question that often offended intercessors and she didn't want to offend Intercessor Sawnell.

High Intercessor Alverez looked to be clouding up, but it was Intercessor Sawnell who answered her question. "We aren't entirely sure. We are fairly confident that there is some sort of agreement between the gods, or some kind of rule imposed on them, that precludes them simply telling us what they want. It doesn't affect other forms of interactions. There are well-documented cases of gods taking on the form of people and animals. But it's equally true that while they are in lesser form they are limited, and even they don't understand the complexities they deal with in their natural state. It's also quite risky, for if a god becomes mortal it can be killed. That's what mortal means, after all."

"All of which makes it very hard for the gods to talk to people in a way that we can understand . . . which brings us back to the signs and portents," Miguel said.

"How do you determine what the signs and portents mean?" Cordelia wondered.

"We guess," High Intercessor Sawnell said. "As I said before. There are rules that we follow to guide our guesses, but basically we guess based on our experience and understanding of the gods."

"And Miguel is guessing that Noron wants him to go along because he got his first spells just after he had decided he should go with me?" Cordelia asked. "I've got to say that seems pretty thin to me."

"I quite agree, young woman," High Intercessor Alvarez said. "Especially considering that Noron is not overly fond of the Kingdom Orcland Trading Company in whose name you acted."

"That's something I wonder about," Cordelia said. "Just how is it you know that Noron isn't overly fond of the KOTC if he doesn't speak to you directly? How do I know that it's not your government who's not overly fond of the KOTC?"

High Intercessor Sawnell coughed and High Intercessor Alvarez shot him a look. "Through the same signs and portents we've been discussing, young woman, delivered with considerable consistency over the last hundred and fifty years. It isn't that the company exists that bothers Noron, but that it fancies itself a government. He, and for that matter, Justain, are also less than pleased at the way the KOTC treats the orcs and other races that come under their sway."

"Honestly, High Intercessor, neither am I. Though I speak as one who knows when I say that at least some of the orc tribes treat orcs much worse than the KOTC does."

"Do you think the fact that others are worse makes the KOTC good?" Alvarez asked, sounding truly interested for the first time in the interview.

"No, I don't. But I was forced to learn that just condemning their actions without offering a workable alternative doesn't do a lot of good."

The High Intercessor nodded.

"And as it happens, the reason Cordelia is going back to the island is because of her obligations to sea elves and lizardmen. Which is another reason that I am convinced that she is doing Noron's and Justain's work," Miguel said.

"Really?" It was clear from High Intercessor Alvarez's tone that he didn't believe that Cordelia was concerned over the sea elves or the lizardmen. "And what do you imagine that you will be able to do for them?"

"I have no idea. We are too far away. I can't tell what they got or what they didn't get. I don't know what I'll be able to do for them. I don't even know that I'll be able to do anything for them. But they are friends who risked their lives on my say-so, so I have to at least go and see what the situation is."

"Tell me now," Miguel said in an irritatingly smug tone, "that this is a quest Noron would disapprove of."

✳ ✳ ✳

The meeting didn't produce much in the way of results. Miguel wasn't forbidden from coming along, nor was the temple of Noron going to fund the quest. He did get a note to other temples of Noron that he was on quest and a legitimate intercessor, provisionally on the business of Noron.

CHAPTER 4

Location: Das Vizart's Dank, Kronisburg
Date: 27 Cashi, 772 AR

"I t'll be about a year," Cordelia told Meggie, a month after she had had her interview with the intercessors. The time between had been spent frantically making magical items. "Because we'll probably end up going all the way around the world. Mostly on ships, but partly on land. It's just the way the winds and currents work. From here we follow the coast of Centraium to the Kingdom Isles, which won't take all that long, about eighteen or twenty days, and then I'm honestly not sure what ship we'll get. It'll depend on what we can afford. We might stop either in KOTC territory or on the southern tip of Amonrai. From there we cross the Great Island Ocean to reach Pango, and from Pango we'll come back to Doichry. The problem is that the currents, and to a great extent, the winds, won't let us go the short way."

Cordelia was packing up her room and putting the things that she wouldn't take with her into storage until she got back. She couldn't afford to pay the rent on the room if she wasn't living in it. Meggie's father allowed that he would let her store her things in an attic room, made secure by a simple spell, so that no one could get at it. Bertie would renew the spell. So all her books were staying behind, except for her spell books. As a book wizard, she had to take those with her. They were necessary for crafting her spells.

"So, if you find another renter, you'll have this room available," Cordelia continued.

"Only if it's another female," Meggie said. "Papa wouldn't rent this room to just anyone, since mine is next door."

"Well, I'm more comfortable putting the big spell safe somewhere no one can get to it. Bertie could, of course, if there's something you need an item for. Generally, though, the longer these items mature, the better they'll be, and I'll probably need to sell a lot of them when I get back. Best not to tempt anyone, I think." Cordelia, as was the habit of many wizards, tended to spend a lot of time making magical items, inlaying them with magic moss, and setting them aside to mature for later sale. It was as much a habit for her as knitting would be to a housewife. And in the last month she had focused almost entirely on laying up a stock of items to mature while she was on her trip. Their sale wouldn't be enough to make up for the costs of the trip, but hopefully it would help.

She gave Meggie a hug, shrugged into her knapsack, and picked up her bottomless bag and tied it to the special belt she had made. That belt helped keep the weight that the bag didn't affect from throwing Cordelia off-balance. Then she turned and left the inn for the ship.

Location: Kronisburg Docks
Date: 28 Cashi, 772 AR

Cordelia and Miguel stood on the aft deck of the *Vindkrof*, a cargo ship that was similar to a galleon or a fluyt, though a bit bigger. It was hard to tell where one plank ended and the next began. Magic made for timbers that fit together better and sometimes they were even grown together.

That, in turn, produced a structure that was both a bit lighter and stronger than such a ship built without magic would have been.

She had three masts and two were square-rigged, the third being fore-and-aft-rigged. She was built to carry the smallest crew and the most cargo that could be managed and this trip was carrying mostly wool from Doichry sheep to Kingdom weavers, and North Bank halibut, presumably to feed those self-same weavers.

She carried twenty officers and gentlefolk and eighty hands. Cordelia and Miguel were among the twenty, Miguel being an intercessor of Noron and Cordelia a wanderer wizard.

"What can you do, girl?" Captain Agusto Darhof asked in an accent that spoke of both Doichry and the Nasine Empire. "I know about intercessors who get spells. We'll never know till it's needed what spells the god has gifted him with, but it'll likely be useful when the time comes. That's up to the gods and mortals have little say. But a wizard is a different matter entirely. I'll be needing a listing of your spells and what they do. Also how long it takes you to craft them."

Cordelia nodded. "I'll write you one, Captain, but I warn you now I have neither weather magic nor a propulsion spell."

"What's a propulsion spell?" Captain Darhof asked.

"I ran into it on a river boat in Amonrai." Cordelia smiled at the captain. "It is cast on the prow of a ship and pulls it in the direction that the caster wants. The one I saw used was about as powerful as a team of two horses, but I assume there are more powerful versions."

"Now that, girl, would be a useful spell," Captain Darhof said. "Is it in the college of wizardry, do you think?"

"I don't know, Captain," Cordelia said. "I hadn't thought of it in years, until I stood on the deck of this ship. My master went to some trouble to acquire it, but his books were lost in the Orclands and I never had it."

"What is it called?"

"I don't know. Tug something or pull something."

"I'll send a message to the college and see if they have anything like what you describe."

"All right." Cordelia wasn't sure what good that would do even if they did. The college of wizardry wasn't exactly free with its collection of spells. No wizard was. Spells were the currency of wizardry and giving them away was much like giving away your fortune.

As it turned out, the college did have a spell that was at least similar. The spell the college had was "as strong as four horses" not the two Cordelia remembered, and Cordelia wasn't sure whether it was a different spell, a different variation on the same spell, or she'd just misremembered how strong it was. Anyway, the whole trip was put back a week while Cordelia was sent back to the college to copy the spell. Not into her spell book, though. Instead she was to make a copy which would belong to Captain Darhof. If she wanted to put it into her spell book, she would have to pay for it. The captain was keeping it and would be able to have any wizard he could hire craft it for him. In theory, those wizards weren't entitled to use it once they left the captain's ship, but everyone knew that they would or at least some of them would, and the college charged the captain accordingly.

They would have preferred to sell the spell to Cordelia, but what good would that do the *Vindkrof* after Cordelia left the ship at Yorkin, the capital city of the Kingdom Isles? So they sold it to Captain Darhof and cautioned him that it shouldn't be tried by a wizard who didn't at least wear the bronze.

It wasn't, Cordelia realized, a very complex spell, comparatively speaking. But it used a lot of power and would work much better crafted into an item. Carrying that amount of magic tied up in knots on your person wasn't comfortable. For pulling a ship, the prow or even the bowsprit would be where you wanted it. After consulting with the ship's carpenter, Cordelia decided on the point where the bowsprit connected to the prow was best. Far enough forward so that the ship would naturally tend to point the direction it was being pulled, but still heavy and strong enough to handle the strain without breaking off. Also it meant that she wouldn't have to climb out on the bowsprit to craft the spell.

"What I need, Filius," Cordelia told the ship's carpenter, "is for you to cut a small groove into the wood where I have made the red chalk marks. See?" Cordelia pointed to the base of the bowsprit where there was a complex spider web of red chalk and a slightly less complex web of blue chalk lines. "Don't worry about the blue lines; they are guides for me in my crafting of the loading spell."

"What's that, miss?" asked Filius, who was about forty and unlettered, but curious about everything and skilled at his trade.

"It's part of how you make a magic item," Cordelia said. "You craft the spell that the magic item will use into it. Then, if you can, you set it aside for a few years. In this case, you would want to set it aside for around thirty years."

"Thirty years! I doubt the *Vindkrof* will still be afloat thirty years from now. She's not fresh off the ways even now."

"I'll take your word for it," Cordelia said. "However, there are all sorts of gradations in magical items and what I propose to do here is to make the weakest sort there is."

"How do you mean?"

"Mostly, all this will be is a place for the wizard to craft the spell into just before she casts it."

"Why do you need that?" Filius asked.

"This isn't a particularly complicated spell, but it has a lot of power. So if I craft it into myself, I have to hold it in place in my head until I am ready to cast it. Even if I am going to cast it as soon as it's crafted, it takes time, concentration and will to craft the spell. Holding magic in place is wearing on the wizard. If I craft it into the bowsprit, that magic is tied into the structure of the enchanted item, not in me. Does that make sense?"

"I see. It's a place to put your tools, rather than holding the awl and the wedge and the file in your hand while you're trying to carve."

"That's it, precisely. If I had to, I could hold the whole spell in my mind, but this will make it possible for an orange wizard, a crafter, to craft the spell. Without this little bit of assistance from what is basically a magical item, most crafters wouldn't have the will to hold it together while they crafted the spell. That's why the college told the captain not to let anyone less than a bronze wizard try it."

Location: Kronisburg Docks
Date: 10 Dugon, 772 AR

Miguel was irritated at the delay. After Cordelia mentioned the tugging spell, the whole project was put back two weeks while Cordelia drew chalk lines on the bowsprit and the ship's carpenter and his apprentices went behind her, carving and shaping. Then Cordelia went behind them, inlaying those lines with her magic moss . . . and during all of this time, they weren't moving. Miguel had come overland from Nasine and he wasn't at all familiar with sea travel. It didn't occur to him that if the wind wasn't blowing, the only way to move the ship was to drop a boat over the side and have men row the boat, pulling the ship behind them. Every sailor on the *Vindkrof* had had blisters on his palms and aches everywhere from pulling this or another ship through the doldrums, places where the wind died.

It was true enough that Miguel was impatient and needed to learn better. It was also true that he didn't at first realize the problem that the spell was meant to address. That changed when he complained once too often to one of the junior officers.

"You find this delay unacceptable, good Intercessor? Let me acquaint you with the alternative. Bosun, lower the starboard boat, if you will. Full crew, less one man. The intercessor is going to row."

Miguel realized that he had put his foot firmly in his mouth. However, he was Nasine, and constitutionally incapable of backing down from a challenge.

Mr. Avery, all of nineteen and a junior officer, wouldn't have arranged this demonstration—no matter how irritating the intercessor had been—except another ship had asked for their help in moving the ship to catch the tide.

"I would be pleased to learn why you feel this is a matter warranting such a delay. And never let it be said that an intercessor of Noron was afraid of a little work."

"Might not be afraid of it," muttered a crewman just on the edge of hearing, "but they all seem allergic to it."

Miguel wisely pretended not to hear.

✳ ✳ ✳

"Pull!"

Miguel pulled. The boat had been lowered and the trip to the *Forgluns* hadn't been particularly difficult. Then they tied a rope to the bowsprit of the *Forgluns* and . . .

Torture. Pulling with all your might and straining every muscle in your body. You pulled and almost nothing happened. To move the ship a few hundred feet—just a few hundred feet—had taken most of a day.

And all Miguel wanted to do now was go somewhere and die. Only his stubborn Nasine pride had held him at the oar.

Location: Kronisburg Docks
Date: 11 Dugon, 772 AR

The next morning, hurting even worse than he had at the end of the rowing, but in much the better graces of the crew, Miguel took himself off to Cordelia and asked if he could help.

"Not unless you can age this thing after we're finished," she said. "This is strictly wizard magic."

That night, Miguel prayed and in the morning he went to the Temple of Noron, and with some of his funds bought a pig for sacrifice. The sacrifice performed, he returned to the ship. The ship's carpenters had finished their work on the bowsprit, and Cordelia was slowly and carefully crafting the filling spell into the carved symbols.

Miguel waited until she was done, then reached out to the bowsprit and cast a spell that Noron had given him. It wasn't a healing spell, and casting it left him exhausted, but at peace.

"What did it do? I see the magic but I can't tell for sure," Cordelia said.

"I don't know. I suspect that it will affect the ageing, but I can't say for sure."

Location: Kronisburg Docks
Date: 12 Dugon, 772 AR

The next morning Cordelia cast the tug boat spell, not from the enchanted bowsprit, but on the prow. She kept it far enough away so that it wouldn't interfere with the enchantment on the bowsprit. She wanted to give whatever Noron and Miguel had done time to work. She had an intuition, and Miguel agreed, that they should allow the spell on the bowsprit to mature for a while.

Meanwhile, now that they were underway, the trip along the northwestern Centraium coast went with little trouble. They had no doldrums to pull through and only one storm, about a week out. Miguel got sick and stayed sick throughout the storm, though it wasn't a particularly bad one.

There were the normal bumps and bruises of a hundred men working at hard dangerous work incurred but—aside from his seasickness—nothing that Miguel couldn't handle. Why the god just left him to suffer through the seasickness Miguel didn't know . . . and Noron wasn't saying.

In surprisingly good time, they made landfall at the mouth of the Yor river and sailed up it for about ten miles to Yorkin, the capital of the Kingdom Isles.

"It's been a good voyage and I thank you for your work on the bowsprit," Captain Darhof said. "And it's good to see an intercessor who is willing to put his back into it when needed," he added with a grin.

Miguel smiled back. "It was a learning experience, Captain. And my back learned well that it isn't fond of me pulling an oar."

"So, you tell me that with the enchantment of the bowsprit, an orange-ranked wizard can craft the thing."

"Yes. But remember two things, Captain. First, not everyone that wears orange embroidery on a wizard's robe can cast orange-level spells. There are a lot of wizards out there who wear robes beyond their abilities. Second, the spell that Miguel cast on the bowsprit seems to be causing the spell to mature more quickly and the longer you wait before you use it, the more benefit you will gain. At least, I think that's what's happening."

"I think so too, Captain. If you can find a wizard who can cast the spell directly, a bronze- or silver-ranked wizard, it would probably be worth the extra cost."

"All that work and time, and I can't use it yet," Captain Darhof complained. "Is magic really worth it?"

"My back says it is," Miguel told him. "My back insists that it's worth it."

CHAPTER 5

Location: Yorkin
Date: 29 Dugon, 772 AR

Yorkin, was the jewel of the Kingdom Isles. Well, it *was*. The Dwarven Empire had had outposts on the island of Wiles and Yorkin had been the major one. When the Empire had started breaking up, the dwarves of Wiles had been left out on their own. The only way to get from the continent to the Isle of Wiles was by ship and dwarves aren't by nature good at seafaring. They had made common cause with their human servants, and—through a series of compromises—a new nation had been born. It was a mostly human nation, but had maintained a place for dwarves and in so doing had gained quite a bit of the dwarven stone working abilities, either from the dwarves themselves or the human apprentices they had taken on.

Yorkin is a city of granite, not wood, and has been from the time it was an outpost of the Dwarven Empire. The docks were stone, the streets were stone, and the buildings were stone. But it was also a human city. There were trees and parks. Wiles is in the temperate zone, but it's an island. The seasons are mild, warm in summer and only cool in winter. It almost never freezes.

And it wasn't freezing today, much to Cordelia's joy. It was nice to be off the ship that smelled of wool and fish.

"So where to now?" Miguel asked.

"Well, we either go looking for lodgings or we go looking for a ship. If we go looking for a ship and don't find one, we'll be sleeping on the street. If we go looking for lodgings, well, we ought to figure on being here for a few days. And we won't be looking for the first ship going in our direction, but for a ship we can hire onto as crew. So it may all take a while. Failing being able to go as crew, we'll need to be concerned about the cost of passage. And there's one other thing I'm concerned about. If I show up on the island of Pango, it's just likely I'll be arrested for unpaid debts. I don't think that would hold up in a Kingdom court, but considering the company governor of Pango, I can't afford to take the chance. I'm going to need a new name. And possibly a disguise."

"Will you pretend not to be a wizard?" Miguel asked, sounding dubious.

"I might. I do think that I should visit the headquarters of the KOTC because I should probably make a report. Not that I expect them to give it much credence. Not after two years and not with a company-warranted lien for owed funds against me." The letter that had started all this was, after all, a letter telling her that she owed Mrs. Amelia Tomson and the lawyers money for the fees incurred in arguing the merits of the prize case on the pirate ship, the *Conquistador*, that she, the sea elves and the lizardmen had captured.

Location: Yorkin
Date: 30 Dugon, 772 AR

"I told you that the KOTC was corrupt," Miguel said when Cordelia stormed out of the company headquarters. He had waited outside. The KOTC was, after all, an enemy to the Nasine Empire.

"Miguel," Cordelia snapped, "back off the preaching. It's becoming annoying, for one thing. Yes, I know what you said. But the company isn't one bit worse than being taken for slaves, which you know as well as I do—or should at least—is exactly what you Nasine were doing to the elves and the orcs a hundred years ago. And you should also know that not all the priests of Noron were sacrificing pigs and cattle when the Nasine Empire controlled the southern tip of Amonrai."

While this was true, it didn't shut Miguel up.

"That was over a hundred years ago."

"Not all of it."

They went back to their lodgings in frosty silence, each having offended the other with the unpalatable truths of their history and the present actions of those in power.

Cordelia was from a province that had only given up slavery a decade before her birth, and many of the provinces of Amonrai still practiced the chattel slavery of elves. But the practices had started with the Nasine Empire, and if they had officially given up the practices—as had the Kingdom and the KOTC—what they had left in its place wasn't a whole lot better. And there were elven and orcish sacrifices made to Noron, Justain, and most of the supposedly good gods. Not often, but it happened and they both knew it.

Location: Yorkin
Date: 5 Coganie, 772 AR

Some days later, when both their tempers had cooled, they decided to get some sightseeing in. After all, how often did two youngsters get to the Jewel of the Kingdom?

They watched the guards marching back and forth in their black and gold livery at the palace of King Robert, then they went to the great temple of Wovoro. Wovoro was the god of sea-faring, a subject near and dear to the hearts of the Kingdom, although Cashi had made inroads into his worship.

The temple of Wovoro was half underground with a tunnel that went out to the sea. There was a great plain of clear stone and on the other side of it the actual ocean came into the building. The altar was placed before the great plain of clear stone, which—legend had it—had been placed there by Wovoro himself. Through the stone, the worshipers could see the depths and the creatures of the depths could see them as well. Sailors were common in the temple, praying for a safe voyage and so were their loved ones left behind praying for their return.

Miguel looked around in wonder and respect. There were greater cathedrals to Noron in Magra, the capital of Nasine, but this was still a wondrous place. Then, spotting one of the intercessors of Wovoro in his green and blue-gray billed cap, he went to speak to him, bowing proper respect as an intercessor of Noron in a temple to another god.

"How can Wovoro help Noron, Intercessor?" the intercessor of Wovoro asked with a raised eyebrow.

"I was wondering what you know of sea elves," Miguel said. "How did they come to be? Were they an act of Wovoro?"

"That's an interesting question. They are well thought of by Wovoro, so the portents suggest anyway, but to the best of our knowledge they were not his work. Why do you ask?"

"A friend of mine is acquainted with some of them and I thought you might know something." Miguel waved Cordelia over and introduced her.

"How did you come to meet sea elves? They are very rare I am told," the intercessor of Wovoro asked.

"I stopped on the Island of Pango on my way to the university of Kronisburg and met them by chance. We worked together well, and I am less than pleased by how they are being treated by the KOTC administration on the island."

"I wasn't aware that there were any sea elves on Pango. Are they followers of Wovoro?"

"I don't know, Intercessor. The subject never came up. The lizardmen that live near them worship an elder dragon as their patron god and creator."

"That is an abomination." The intercessor of Wovoro had lost his smile. "That they worship a dragon?"

"That they exist at all," the intercessor said. "They were indeed created by an elder dragon, so that he might have tasty snacks. When a dragon feeds, it feeds on the magic as well as the meat. That's why he made them intelligent. Greater intelligence, more magic."

"That may be true, Intercessor, but it is hardly their fault. And however they came to be, they are. And as intelligent beings they deserve respect, don't they?"

The intercessor gave Cordelia a hard look. "A wolf may kill out of hunger, not evil intent, but the child it eats is just as dead. Granted, it's not their fault . . . but the fault is in them, bred into their bones by the dragon that made them. You would be wise to stay away from them, lest the corruption infect you as well."

Miguel realized that this wasn't going anywhere he wanted to go, so quickly changed the subject. "About the sea elves, Intercessor. Does the temple of Wovoro have a policy about how they should be treated?"

"They are elves but they are of the sea and the province of Wovoro and shouldn't be disturbed or abused," the intercessor of Wovoro said, still testily. "But the temple has little authority over the KOTC."

The trip to the temple of Wovoro was disappointing in that it didn't actually help them much at all. But the place itself was enchantingly beautiful.

Location: Yorkin
Date: 6 Coganie, 772 AR

"We have a ship," Cordelia told Miguel the next day. "It won't be leaving for a week but we can move aboard any time. That tug spell is really useful." Cordelia had quietly copied the tug spell into her spell book. And felt a bit guilty about it. But not so guilty that she wasn't going to use it if she needed it. Partly that was because she felt that the spell was properly hers anyway since it had been in Rojer's spell book. But mostly she figured that she would go ahead and buy the spell after she got back to the college. She continued her explanation. "The *Costoga* is going to Arginia in Amonrai, not the port of Goodlanding in the Orclands, but that's probably for the best, since the KOTC headquarters declined to void the notice of indebtedness. They won't try to enforce it now, where I could appeal to a Kingdom court that would throw the thing out. But Governor Andrew Hopkins of Pango has too many friends to let it be quashed."

"So you figure on going to Pango in disguise, but what does that have to do with preferring Amonrai to the port of Goodlanding?"

"Because I won't have to go into disguise till we get to Amonrai. We won't be on a KOTC ship on the trip from here to Arginia in Amonrai. And that means that I can go as a wizard and pay my way with the tug spell, which is why we are going to be here another week. In a long sea voyage like this we are almost certain to have periods of calm and we'll need the spell. You, not being wanted by the KOTC, can hire on as an intercessor with healing spells. But once I stop being a wizard, I am going to have to pay for my passage and that's expensive."

The next week was busy but not particularly interesting. Cordelia and the carpenters on the *Costoga* enchanted the *Costoga*'s bowsprit and Miguel spent most of the time going around talking religion with the intercessors of Yorkin, including intercessors of Noron. Worship of Noron was legal, but not generally popular in the Kingdom Isles, though he was more popular among the soldiers than the general populace. Still, there were temples of Noron in Yorkin and Miguel visited them all, and did healings and pronounced blessings—all the things that an intercessor with spells is expected to do.

Location: Costoga, Yorkin
Date: 14 Coganie, 772 AR

"So this thing will drag us out of the harbor?" Captain Rochester asked, sounding doubtful. She was a short woman with a fair amount of extra weight on her, but strong and solid-looking. She smoked a fancy pipe with the image of a bearded man on the bowl and pointed with the stem.

"No. *I* will tug us out of the harbor. The enchantment is just to hold the spell. In the future, almost any competent orange-level crafter wizard will be able to use the spell, assuming he has it in his book. Of course, if you want to purchase a ship's copy, we can work something out."

"So you've said," Captain Rochester growled. "Meanwhile, I've yet to see the thing work."

So, having already crafted the spell into the enchanted bowsprit, Cordelia cast it and slowly, very slowly, the ship began to move. A team of four horses is fairly strong, strong enough in fact to move a three hundred ton ship. But not strong enough to move that ship very fast. A man walking with a cane could have out-distanced them. Still, the captain was impressed, because she understood what it meant.

"And you'll be able to do this," the captain asked, "how often?"

"Once, perhaps twice, a day for four hours at a stretch. The spell takes about an hour and a half to craft and, if not adjusted, will pull always in the direction that the bowsprit is pointing. Mostly that should do what you need. If there's heavy weather, I can adjust the direction of the pull, but it's not easy." Cordelia was being less than completely honest when she said that last. There wasn't any real difficulty in changing the direction; she just didn't want to spend her days acting as a secondary steersman for the ship.

Soon enough they were under sail and the little bit of extra oomph that the tug spell provided became superfluous. Still, as soon as the spell wore out, Cordelia crafted a new one into the bowsprit, but she didn't activate it. It would last a little while, not for very long, and as long as it was there it would keep the enchantment stable.

"Well," Captain Rochester said, walking up to Cordelia, "I guess you're right. It did get us out of harbor. We probably need to talk about this."

"It's a useful spell, Captain. More useful than I realized when I first saw it on a ferry boat on the Mosoris River years ago. I do have ink with me . . ."

"Maybe. We'll see how it goes over the course of the trip. You're talking a lot of money for something that I can't use myself, but have to hire someone to use. I might do just as well to look for a wizard that already has the spell."

"Indeed you might. But if you have it, you can sell the right to copy it to a wizard who comes to work for you."

This discussion would be repeated on and off in many variations all the way to Arginia, which took only about twenty-five days. Captain Rochester eventually decided not to purchase a copy of the tug spell. She was determined to find wizards who already had the spell and hire them.

Cordelia suspected that Captain Rochester was a bit short of cash. Well, that was all right. Cordelia wished her good luck in finding a wizard who could cast it and even suggested that she look among pilot wizards on the river boats. "After all, that's where I first saw it."

It was a reasonable end to a somewhat tedious voyage.

Location: Arginia, Southern Amonrai
Date: 5 Justain, 773 AR

"So where do we go?" Miguel asked.

"How should I know? I've never been here."

"You're from Amonrai."

"And you're from Centriaum, so you can tell me how to navigate the central jungles?"

"All right, all right. But where do we go?"

It was, unfortunately, a good question. They knew a little about the city from geography studies in the university. It was one of the major cities of Amonrai. The city of Arginia, located at the mouth of the Amo River, was legally two cities in two provinces, one on the north side of the river and one on the south side. There wasn't a great deal of difference between the two in terms of culture but they answered to two different hierarchies all the way up to the provincial level.

On the ship they had learned a bit more, and that bit was the sort of thing that didn't usually make it into geography books.

"The local constabulary," one of the crew told Cordelia, "they get along all right on the big things like murder and treason and such. But they find it right convenient to not be able to chase criminals across the river. The city guards on the south side wear a light brown tunic and the guards on the north side wear a light blue tunic. So if you see a light blue tunic on the south side, you mostly don't have to worry none."

"So why don't they set up a way of coordinating?"

"What?" the crewman had laughed. "And lose all the bribes they get from the cut purses and the like that live on one side of the river and ply their trades on the other?" He shook his head. "Everyone knows how it works and everyone makes their payments. Otherwise the guard forces get suddenly cooperative."

The *Costoga* was docked on the south side of the bay but there was regular boat traffic across the river, which was from one hundred to five hundred feet wide in the city. There was also a bridge built across one of the narrower bits. It was a tall bridge. Cordelia could see it from where she stood on the *Costoga*'s deck next to the gangplank. She knew that bridge was a point of pride to both halves of the city, it having been built using a combination of muscle and magic, and a three-masted schooner could sail under it without losing a mast. There were shops of all sorts in Arginia and everything was for sale. Everything.

Miguel and Cordelia set out walking, hoping to find decent lodging away from the river and the noise of the crowds. They had been walking for over an hour when they turned a corner and inadvertently walked into a slave auction. There were elves for sale in the market and the auctioneer was proclaiming the value of his merchandise in a loud, booming voice.

"O'ya O'ya," the auctioneer half-shouted half-sang. "We have for you today a young male, good for years of hard work before he has to be treed!"

The bidding started in a desultory manner and the young elf stood quietly, head bowed, long, straight blond hair hiding most of his face, just the tips of his pointed ears sticking out. He was wearing a loincloth that barely managed the minimum necessary for modesty. And, to Cordelia's eye, he had no expression on his face at all. His shoulders, however, spoke of dejection. He was sold for two hundred reali. Cordelia didn't know or want to know if that was a good price. He was led away.

"O'ya O'ya," the auctioneer half-shouted half-sang again. "A breeding female!" Fresh from the tree and ready to be used. In prime condition. And let me tell you, her owner was loath to let her go."

The bidding this time was a bit more spirited, though the elven woman who might be twenty or two thousand depending on how many times she had been restored by a tree, was just as quiet and passive as the elven lad had been. Cordelia thought she was probably older. She had that ageless quality that some elves get. Nothing really matters, this too will pass. She brought four hundred reali and was led away by a well-dressed but quite unattractive young human with crooked teeth and a leering grin.

"O'ya O'ya, here we have a child not yet treed, good for the fine work of weaving." The child only brought eighty-three reali.

Cordelia and Miguel stood entranced by the spectacle, unable to look away, Cordelia, remembering Aradrel and imagining him up on that block being sold.

"O'ya O'ya, here we have a natural wizard. He's been tested and certified. We have his papers. This one can make you simple magical items to use or sell and he's young enough to train to your preferences."

The auctioneer winked at the crowd, and suddenly Cordelia was sure that he was pointing out that the boy, an elven lad who looked to be about fourteen, was powerful enough in magic to make a good sacrifice if that was what the buyer wanted him for. Or for a partial sacrifice, and then stick him in a tree for a few years to grow back. The first was illegal anywhere in the civilized world, but still practiced. The second, though . . . the second was probably legal here.

Cordelia wanted to throw up. She wanted to burn the place to the ground and the city with it, but there was nothing she could do. So she did nothing at all as the boy was sold to an elderly man in wizard's robes with purple embroidery that described him as an item wizard, the sort who couldn't hold a complicated spell in his head, but could craft incredibly complicated spells into various magical items and possibly could actually craft those magical items.

It was obvious to Cordelia what the boy was going to be used for. His magical talent, perhaps even his life force, because the distinction between the two was pretty iffy, would be poured into magical items created by the wizard to age them. Perhaps not enough to kill the boy, but enough to stunt him, almost certainly. And there wasn't a thing Cordelia could do about it.

"Let's get out of here," she told Miguel. "I'm going to be sick."

Miguel gulped. "So am I."

They got some hard looks as they hurried away from the auction. Apparently even looking disapproving was unacceptable.

They headed for the river and took a boat to the north side, hoping—but not really expecting—it would be different.

CHAPTER 6

Location: Arginia, Southern Amonrai
Date: 5 Justain, 773 AR

The rooming house was five blocks from the river and dirty.
Literally dirty. There was filth everywhere and the room stank.
They got it for two reali a week and two weeks in advance, if you
please. There were no locks on the door, just a latch, and the man who ran
the place smelled of old drink and not enough trips to the baths.

"I can't believe this disgusting mess is worth two reali a week," Cordelia
said. "He's taking advantage of us, and you know it as well as I do."

"Certainly, he is," Miguel said. "But it's the cheapest rooming house on
this side of the river and I'm tired of walking. Besides, you know that you
can fix this."

Cordelia glared at him. "I'm supposed to be disguising myself here,
remember?" Then she looked around the room again and sighed. "But I
can't live in this." Cordelia pulled the two servant amulets from her pouch
and set them to work. A servant spell—or a servant amulet, which is the
same thing—is, when it comes down to it, simply a force.

"Sure. But first be Cordelia, then disguise yourself," Miguel said. "Get
the clothing you'll wear, but don't wear it out of the room. You were
wearing wizard robes under your elven cloak when we arrived, so the old

drunk saw you in them. All we need to do now is not let him see you leave dressed in your new clothing."

Miguel looked at her critically. "You might consider cutting your hair. And perhaps lightening it a bit. That would probably make a difference."

"My hair?" Cordelia was aghast. Her hair was black, long and silky and she had long considered it her best feature.

"Hair grows," Miguel pointed out.

"Argh." Cordelia knew that was the truth, but she still didn't like it much. In spite of which, the next day she visited the baths and had it cut and lightened. It did make a difference in her appearance. And she bought a hat to hide the new hair from the landlord, as well as new clothing for her disguise.

She bought women's working pants, the sort that a sailor or a field hand from up north might wear. Down here, the field hands were almost exclusively elven slaves. She also bought a shirt and jacket, along with sturdy boots.

She would put away her elven cloak when she took on the new character of Anne Brooks for the voyage to Pango Island. Meanwhile, she simply wore her wizard robes, and when it was chilly, her elven cloak and boots, along with her new hat, which hid the hair she had had lightened to a sandy blond.

All this took just under a week of running errands and collecting the kit of a traveling woodworker. Cordelia was a bit tired of having to think about all the things she needed to do. So, having put together the disguise, and Miguel being off searching for a temple to ply his trade, she decided to go to a play. She would go as Cordelia Cooper, wandering wizard, except for the hat, which would hide her now-blonde hair.

The name of the play was *Our Kingdom Relations*, and it was billed as a hilarious comedy of Kingdom Isles decadence and conflict with Amonraian practicality. Cordelia, in spite of the fact that she was wearing her elven cloak because of the chilly air and her wizard robes which indicated a certain status, bought one of the cheap seats because she was still on a budget.

Location: Arginia, Southern Amonrai
Date: 12 Justain, 773 AR

Jimmy Dugan followed his friend into the box, laughing and singing, a bottle of good Korkin brandy clutched in his hand. It had been a good day, today. His group of fellows had spent it drinking and carousing, eating and drinking, wandering and watching, and generally having a high old time. All he really needed to top off the day was a willing woman—or even one not so willing. Jimmy didn't care which.

He looked over at Young Master Charles Adrogo, the son of Master Antonio Adrogo, who owned over a thousand acres of prime bottomland and over two hundred elves, with an inebriated mix of affection and resentment. Charley was his friend as long as Jimmy kept his place, and it was Charley's money that paid for the good Korkin brandy and the evening at the theater, and that would pay for their trip to the gambling houses after the theater and persuade or hire some girls into their beds. Jimmy was thankful for that money and resentful that he had none of his own.

Jimmy looked around the theater, down at the hoi polloi, where he would be watching the play if it weren't for Charley. There . . . that was strange. An elven cloak? They didn't let elves into the theater and wearing an elven cloak was tasteless at best. It was a slap in the face to every right-thinking human.

"Charley, look!" he said, pointing. "Probably some northerner making common cause with the elves."

"Maybe," Charley said, clearly unconvinced. "Or it could just be someone who likes elven cloaks. Not very stylish, I'll grant, but nothing to get upset about."

For the rest of the play, which wasn't very good—the writing was poor and the acting was worse, overblown and stiff all at the same time—Jimmy Dugan felt his eye constantly returning to the elven cloak and its wearer. When intermission finally came around, he saw why she had been let in. She was wearing wizard's robes. But what was a proper book wizard doing wearing an elven cloak?

The hawkers were passing through the audience, selling popped corn and crab cakes in perin sauce. And the girl—he thought it was a girl—had flipped her cloak back and displayed the silver strands of embroidery and the orange, as well. *Now, wait just one minute*, Jimmy thought. *Silver embroidery or orange, but not both.*

There was something wrong here. And suddenly Jimmy knew what it was. She was an elf, trying to pass. Probably had some human blood in her, which would explain why she was stocky, not elven thin. But Jimmy figured that she was a natural wizard and that was, in Jimmy's mind, a sure sign of elven blood. And they were on the north side of the river. Here, in this place, any elven blood at all made you an elf and it was a crime to try and pass as human. Then it hit him. An elven mage was a prime slave. A good elven mage could be worth over a thousand reali and the fellow who exposed a passing elf would get the price it brought at auction.

For the rest of the performance, Jimmy watched the elf like a hawk. There was no way he was going to let her get away. He wasn't sure what to do about Charley. On the one hand, there was no way he wanted to share the reward with Charley. Charley didn't need it, after all. But a wizard, even an elven wizard, was nothing to mess around with.

Finally the play ended and he, with some difficulty, managed to get Charley to accompany him to look at the oddity of someone in an elven cloak attending a play. Elves shouldn't be watching a human play. Elves were just dull. Dull and stupid and slow. They needed those long lives to produce something that looked like wit. That's why they gloried in slow, intricate melodies. Their brains didn't work fast enough for real music.

* * *

Cordelia had flipped up the left side of her elven cloak, displaying her wizard robes with the silver and orange embroidery and pulled back the hood exposing her hat. Partly, it was habit. She had learned to display her robes in Kronisburg.

The last thing Cordelia would have expected at any time was someone actually grabbing her by the shoulders and pulling her hat off her head. It generally was considered a bad idea to lay hands on a wizard. Most people tended to step aside when they saw someone in wizard robes. So being jerked around as though she were someone's donkey frightened her. She froze.

"See?" the idiot who had pulled her around shouted. "I told you she was an elf!" The idiot pointed at her hair. "See? She's even blonde."

The crowd were all looking at her and Cordelia didn't have a clue what he was going on about or why. It didn't occur to her to remember that in southern Amonrai even a little elven blood made you an elf and she didn't know that elves were required to carry proof of their status as free persons lest they be enslaved.

"Get your hands off me, you cretin!" Cordelia said. "I'm no more an elf than you are."

"See? She even talks like an elf."

Then another voice, from a tall, dark man with a goatee and coal-black, curly hair, said, "We'd better see your papers, girl."

"What papers?" Cordelia asked.

"Proof of liberty or ownership papers, girl. You know the law." The bearded man was sounding impatient now. *Well,* thought Cordelia, *that makes us a matched set. I've about had enough of these idiots.*

"I am a citizen of Fornteroy Province."

"Oh, great," the first one said. "A damned northern elf. Them northerners are always practicing miscegenation and the like. That explains why she's so fat. She's a part-elf, sure as Justain's a lawgiver.

"I claim her. You're my witness, right, Charley?"

"Sure," the other one said. "If she's from Fornteroy, she should know better."

"You can't—" Then Cordelia's response was interrupted as the first one grabbed her arm. "Are you insane?" she started to say, but he was trying to twist her arm up behind her back and it hurt. At this point, Cordelia wasn't irritated any more. She was scared, very scared, and remembering orcish arms manhandling her. She didn't think at all. She pointed her finger at him and invoked Wizard Bolt. By now that spell had long been a part of her and she could fire it a half a dozen times in as many seconds.

A lance of magic went from her finger to his head. He didn't even scream. He just collapsed to the ground. "What kind of an idiot lays hand on a wizard?" she shouted.

"Here, there . . ." the black-haired one stopped as his friend fell to the ground. He looked to the man on the ground, then to her, back to the man on the ground, and his hand went to the sword at his hip. "You killed him," he shouted. "You killed him, you elven whore."

Then he charged, sword extended. "Charge" might be overstating things a bit because he made less than a single step before Cordelia put a wizard bolt into his chest. And when he didn't go down, she followed it up with another.

"She killed Charles Adrogo," shouted someone. Then the crowd pulled back and there was a space around her, as if she were contagious.

"Who is Charles Adrogo?"

"His father will have your head, elf, wizard or no. His papa will kill you." A murmur of agreement rose in the crowd.

Cordelia hid her fright. She'd been involuntarily involved in the deaths of more than one scion of a wealthy family. Although it hadn't exactly been her idea, it had still happened. And in her experience, justification or even innocence didn't cut a lot of ice with the grieving family.

Cordelia decided that she probably didn't want to hang around to wait for the local constabulary. She turned and ran, pointing her finger here and there, but not actually invoking Wizard Bolt. It wasn't necessary. The pointed finger got them moving out of her way.

Three blocks later, she ducked into an alley and tried to think. She knew several spells that might help but she didn't have any of the really good ones crafted. All she had crafted was Hide Me, which only worked if you stayed still. If she had had Lighten Me crafted she could make herself light as a feather and jump to the roof of the building. She could create a temporary set of ethereal wings, though she hadn't used the Wings spell enough to have learned to fly well. But she didn't have that spell crafted either. She could grease an axle if she needed to, because that spell was internalized like Wizard Bolt, but that wouldn't do her any good.

No one in the crowd would come after her, she thought, well, hoped. On the other hand, it was a safe bet that someone in the crowd would report the incident to the authorities. Cordelia started moving as quickly and as quietly as she could back toward the boarding house. If she could get there, she could craft something to help her get out of this city. Besides, she needed to get with Miguel. She wondered if anyone in the crowd would recognize her and know where she lived. She thought back, trying to remember if she'd ever used her name or where she was staying. She couldn't remember exactly, but she didn't think she had.

* * *

Cordelia slipped around to the back of the boarding house. There was a back entrance that was less used than the front. She took off her elven cloak, then quietly slipped up the stairs, remembering only at the last moment that she wasn't wearing her hat. It had been lost at the theater.

It didn't matter. Nobody saw, nobody noticed, and nobody cared. She got back to her room, took off her wizard robes and put on her disguise. She then sat down and started crafting Wings. She almost decided on Lighten Me, but Wings lasted longer even if she did fly like a drunken albatross.

Miguel wasn't back yet, so she packed for herself and for him, then waited impatiently, and thought about what other spells she should prepare. She also decided that during the next voyage, she was going to work on figuring out just which spells she needed to have internalized. Grease, for instance, she needed to let fade away. And Cornishain's Ageing. If she needed to age something, she could craft it. What she needed for internalized spells were spells that she would need in an emergency. And that was another problem. Cordelia couldn't just decide to internalize a spell. It didn't work that way. Spells got internalized by use. To internalize a spell, she needed to use it every day. Once it was internalized, she could keep it that way by focusing on it for a few minutes a day without having to invoke it, but to get it internalized took work.

So on the ship she would have to come up with a list of spells she wanted to make part of her, and exercise herself on them till she had them solid. That was going to be pretty obvious and she wondered how the captain and crew were going to react to her throwing tongues of flame or lightning bolts around for practice. She wasn't sure she'd put Wings into her list. Flying like a drunken albatross over the open ocean might not be a really good idea. On the other hand, if she got enough practice, being able to fly around near a ship would be really useful for things like seeing pirates before they saw her ship, or finding the coast and directing the ship to it.

Oh, well. She'd have time to think about that later. Meanwhile, where was Miguel? She needed to get out of this city, whether he did or not.

* * *

Miguel whistled as he walked back down the street leading to the boarding house. He had been talking about swordsmanship with some of the followers of Noron at the local temple and time had gotten a little away from him. Intercessors of Noron were not expected to be the quiet, contemplative sorts that became intercessors of Timu or Barra. Noron was a god of contest and contestants needed to be fit. So conversation had led to practice and time had gotten even more away from him, but he was replete with the sort of good soreness that came from a good workout and pleased at how well his skills had shown themselves.

He came in and saw the landlord drunk, and sighed, but went up the stairs with good heart. Everything was fine, in fact, until he opened the door to the room he shared with Cordelia and found her dressed in her disguise and their bags packed. Almost before this state of affairs had registered, Cordelia was on him, asking, "Where have you been?"

"At the weapons hall," Miguel said. "In the Temple of Noron. Why? What's happened?"

"I killed a man tonight. Two of them. I was attacked, accused of being an elf, as though that were some sort of crime—which I guess it is here—but when one of them grabbed me, I shot him with a wizard bolt. Then the other pulled a sword on me."

"Have you gone to the authorities?"

"Apparently," Cordelia told him with clearly strained patience, "the second one, the one with the sword, was the son of some sort of powerful local. I somehow don't think I would get a fair hearing."

"Cordelia," Miguel said, with as much patience as he could muster, "from what you describe, it was a fair contest. You will certainly not be faulted since they attacked you. Even if it is fairly clear they were mentally deficient, bringing a sword to a wizard duel. So, you must put your trust in the authorities. It's how we remain civilized. So we should go to them, right now and explain."

Cordelia looked at him like he was crazy for a moment, then her expression softened. "Miguel, do you remember what happened when Lord Karl was killed by the lich?"

"Well, vaguely. I understand that his father was quite unreasonable about the whole matter, but that makes my point. The authorities at the university supported you, didn't they?"

"I am a wanted criminal in Lord Karl's home county, and that when I was fighting on his side, on his instigation, and just happened to be there when he got killed by an evil undead monster. This time, I personally killed the drunken sot who attacked me with a sword. I don't know how powerful this planter is, but from what the crowd was saying, he's plenty powerful enough to have me killed. And I don't propose to risk my life on his good humor."

Miguel stopped, taken aback by Cordelia's position. It was wrong, he knew it had to be wrong, but at the same time he couldn't help but understand her logic. After struggling with what his beliefs said was right and what logic told him was right, he finally yielded to another point. This was Cordelia's quest so it was her decision, as he had agreed when he joined her. "What do you want to do then?"

"I want to find a ship and get out of this city and out of this province," Cordelia said. "And I want to do it as fast as we can, before any one figures out who the elven wizard that killed the planter's son actually was."

With grave doubts that he was doing the right thing, Miguel went along with Cordelia's plan, such as it was. They made their way out of the rented room and down toward the harbor.

Miguel took the lead down the street that fronted the harbor, and a few blocks later, they saw some guards with torches stopping people. Cordelia ducked into an alley while Miguel went forward to ask the guard what was going on.

"Well, you're not the elven wizard," one of the guards said with a grin.

"Shut up, Bobby," the other said.

"Have you seen an elven wizard about six foot tall, perhaps taller, blond hair and an elven cloak with orange and silver on it and wizard robes? She killed the son of a planter in cold blood."

"Why?" Miguel asked.

"Why what?"

"Why did this elven wizard kill the son of a planter?"

"Who knows why elves do anything? Maybe she wanted him and he wasn't interested. You know how elves are."

"No, actually. I am from Nasine. We don't have a lot of elves there. What are elves like?"

"Weeelll," Bobby started.

"Shut it, Bobby," the other guard repeated. "We don't have time for your dirty stories."

Miguel passed on, trying not to shake his head over the absurdity of it all, and found himself wondering who they would find to fit that description. For he was very much afraid that they would find someone. That bothered him rather a lot and yet the whole interview had thoroughly supported Cordelia Cooper's claim that she couldn't expect a fair hearing.

* * *

This alley found Cordelia much better prepared than the last had. She had Wings prepared and Lighten Me, as well. Like Lighten Sword or Lighten Mace, Lighten Me didn't affect a person's force, but let the person move as though they weighed about as much as a feather. She cast the spell on herself and with two quick steps leaped to the top of the building she was standing next to. Lighten Me lasted rather less time than Lighten Sword, but she managed to skip from roof top to roof top and bypass the guardsmen. Three blocks later, she landed heavily in another alley, then stepped out to rejoin Miguel and asked him what he had learned.

"You're in little danger, Cordelia, but I would hate to be an elf in this town tonight."

"I'd hate to be an elf in this town anytime," Cordelia said.

CHAPTER 7

Location: Arginia, Southern Amonrai
Date: 13 Justain, 773 AR

Getting to the harbor didn't solve their problems. The harbor wasn't exactly closed down at sunset, because shipping was dependent on the tides. But mostly people tried to schedule their business in daylight hours so the night shift was more like a watch than a do.

"Miguel, you go to the harbor master's office and see what ships are leaving. I'll wait here. Even if the description they've got of me is totally off the mark, it's better if I am not seen."

"All right," Miguel agreed. "I'll be back soon."

Miguel headed for the harbor master's office, still concerned about the morality of their actions. At this time of the night, the harbor master's office was a quiet place. It was occupied by one older gentleman who seemed inordinately busy brewing a pot of something. Whatever it was, it smelled quite good. Miguel cleared his throat to get the old fellow's attention.

"What do you need, sonny?" then, apparently noticing Miguel's hat, "Oh sorry, Intercessor. How can I help you?"

"I'm looking to crew on a ship heading west and I'm in a hurry."

"Her father caught you did he?" The old man cackled. "Well, Intercessor, unless the gods decide to make a special effort on your behalf . . ." The old fellow paused and looked at Miguel, "Nasine, are you?"

"Yes, I am, harbor master. And an intercessor of Noron," Miguel said, still a bit incensed at the harbor master's insinuation. Not at the thought that he might be doing something with a young woman that her father might catch them at, but at the thought that he would run away. That feeling of outrage was in no way diminished by the fact that he was, in fact, running away—or at least helping Cordelia run away and going with her. Miguel wasn't stupid; he knew that sometimes you had to make a tactical retreat, but knowing and feeling are two different things.

However, Miguel's outrage didn't seem to bother the harbor master at all. "In that case, maybe you do have reason to get somewhere, rather than to be away from here." The old man held up a hand as Miguel started to bristle. "Not that it matters to me either way, sonny. Not my business either way and I never was the curious sort. I have respect for privacy, I have.

"Anyway, there's a Nasinen-flagged three-masted freighter called the *Maranho* that's sailing on the morning tide for the Nasine colony out west. That one sails on the morning tide, which will be in about six hours, two hours before dawn.

"On the other hand, the *Prince Carlos* is sailing directly for the Nasine territory in the Orc Lands. *Prince Carlos* leaves day after tomorrow, but will get you to the Orc Lands colony sooner, a lot sooner.

"Now, personally, I can't imagine why anyone would want to travel to a trading colony full of wild elves in preference to a relatively civilized colony in the Orc Lands, where they at least keep the orcs under control. But if it should happen that you want to take the *Maranho* instead of the *Prince Carlos*, it's docked in the south harbor, which will entail crossing the bridge. Now, if her daddy don't have guards on the bridge, you should have plenty of time. Being a Nasine ship and you an intercessor of Noron, shouldn't be no problem to get a berth aboard, though I doubt they'll have crew work for you."

"Noron grants me spells," Miguel said, though why he cared what this old man thought was beyond him.

"At your age?" The old man grinned. "The fighter must be losing it!" Then he laughed at Miguel's expression. "Off with you now, lad, and see you avoid her outraged papa on the way."

* * *

"There is a Nasine freighter leaving from the south harbor at around four in the morning. Positioned as the harbor is, the tides are especially important. The problem is I'm sure that the guards will be watching for you on the bridge and even if the descriptions are lousy, someone might get lucky."

"Well, if you can make the arrangements, I can fly out to the ship. Wings or, more precisely, Adreana's Gossamer Wings spell. I crafted it before I left the room."

Miguel nodded. Going to school with a wizard college next door was a broadening experience. He had seen people flying around on magical wings fairly often. "Fine, but how will you find the ship? Especially in the dark?"

Cordelia paused and thought, then she reached into the back pack and pulled out the Bottomless Bag. She pulled one of the light crystals that she had gotten so many years ago in the elven caves. It was the brighter of the two and a fairly bright light. "Here is what you do. If there is a problem, come back and tell me about it but if everything is worked out and the way is prepared just stay on the ship. Once the ship is out of the harbor, show this from the poop-deck." Then she considered again, and brought out the other light crystal. "Better yet, hold them both up. That way it will be hard for me to miss."

* * *

Miguel had no trouble crossing the bridge and not much finding the ship. On the ship, however, everyone but the watch was asleep and no one was willing to wake the captain, because it had been a busy day getting ready to sail and their morning was starting before dawn. Besides which, the captain wasn't the least bit happy with those who woke him in the middle of the night for no greater reason than that a boy intercessor wanted to have a chat.

"Look, Intercessor, I know that it's important to you, but it will wait till the captain is ready to hear you. You can wait on board and I don't doubt that the captain will agree to give you passage, you being on Noron's business and all. But you'll need to be able to bring him down in person to get me to wake the captain after the day we had. Sorry, but that's just the way it goes."

"I need—"

"It'll have to wait."

Miguel gave up and waited, worried all the while that the captain would refuse—not so much refuse Miguel, but refuse Cordelia. Cordelia, after all, was the one who was wanted. Still, there was nothing to do but wait.

Location: The Maranho, Arginia, Southern Amonrai
Date: 13 Justain, 773 AR

Captain Batuca was woken by his steward at seven bells of the mid-watch. Pedro handed him a warm cup of the bean tea that they drank here.

It tasted as foul as it smelled good. But it woke him up, given a little time. They would be pulling out in only a little while, so he quickly dressed and headed for the quarterdeck.

He stepped out of his cabin door and looked around at the night. There were a few lights from the city, but not that many and the morning fog was starting to roll in. Then he saw the boy. sleeping on his quarterdeck. "Who . . . ?" He stopped, recognizing the intercessor's hat that was tilted at an angle on the lad's—no, the intercessor's—head.

"Who is this, then?" he asked the ensign who had the midwatch.

"I don't really know, sir. He came aboard during Commander Flanders watch and the commander said to leave him for you. He wants passage, I think."

"Well, wake him and find out, Ensign."

"Aye, sir."

Ensign Crus went over and, a little timidly, shook the intercessor's shoulder, while Captain Batuca watched with amusement, curiosity and a spicing of concern. When an intercessor of any god, much less Noron, was sleeping on your quarterdeck, it meant that things could get interesting. Captain Batuca wasn't sure he wanted an interesting experience in these waters, but the gods gave what the gods gave. He was also more than a little pressed for time if he wanted his ship towed out to catch the tide and have some sea room when the winds shifted.

The intercessor woke, mumbling, then looked around and saw him. "Sorry to be sleeping on your quarterdeck, Captain . . . ?"

"Batuca."

"Captain Batuca. I arrived last night after you had retired and your crew was in terror of disturbing your rest."

"As they ought to be. What do you need of me, Intercessor?"

"As to that, passage to the Elfsain, and possibly beyond that. I am gifted by Noron of spells which will likely be of value to your crew as the voyage progresses. I can work my passage and . . ."

"Fine, fine. We'll work out the details later. Right now, I have to get this ship ready to move. Just stay out of everyone's way for the next couple of hours and we'll see to the rest later."

"But—"

"Not now, Intercessor!" Captain Batuca said, seeing the ship's boat hanging up rather than lowering. "Back there, men. Pull her up and clear the line." Captain Batuca ran forward, totally forgetting the intercessor.

* * *

Miguel stood, mouth opened to tell the Captain about Cordelia and the fact that she would be joining them once the ship was out of the harbor. But there was no captain to tell. Perhaps Noron was suggesting that mention of that little detail could wait.

"Intercessor," the ensign—Miguel didn't know his name—said. "We're going to be very busy here on the quarterdeck for the next little while. If you'll go up that ladder to the poop-deck and wait there or on the fantail, I'm sure the captain will have time for you once we have sea room."

Miguel did as he was told and checked the two Jewels of Light in his pouch. The fantail or the poop deck would probably be an excellent place to display the lights for Cordelia to see.

* * *

Cordelia, after Miguel left, had spent a few minutes standing in the alley and trying to figure out her best option. She had used her Lighten Me spell already, but that wasn't the only way to climb a wall. She was perfectly capable of climbing a wall the old-fashioned way, assuming she could find the handholds she needed. She paced down the alley, looking for a place to climb.

Nothing. Someone had apparently gone to some trouble to see to it that she couldn't climb their building. Which made perfect sense, for all that Cordelia was looking for was a comfortable place to wait, there were no doubt those who were looking for a way in so that they might steal. Cordelia was going to have to find a place where the owners weren't so careful. That took her almost half an hour and almost got her spotted.

Eventually she found a building with a broken drain spout that allowed her the handholds that she needed. She climbed up to the roof of a building only a couple of blocks from the harbor. It was a slate roof and moderately steep, so a comfortable perch wasn't easy. But she found herself a nook where she didn't think she would slip, and proceeded to wait. It would be hours before Miguel got back and even longer if everything went well and he sent the signal. Concern kept her awake. Concern, both that she might miss him if he came back and that she might miss the signal. This plan to get them on board a ship, was starting to seem like a really bad idea.

Suddenly Cordelia grinned to herself. She felt that way every time. After the plan was made and put into motion, but before it had come to fruition, she always felt like it was all going to go wrong. Then her smile faded. Sometimes it did all go wrong.

Several hours later, in spite of her concern, her eyelids were drooping. She looked up at the sky, trying to judge the time by the constellations, then looked out at the harbor. Ships were starting to bustle in the dark harbor. Lamps were lit and boats were going over the sides of ships. It must be getting close to the tide turning or it had already started to turn and ships were trying to catch the ebbing tide to pull them out to sea. She looked to the south in the hopes of seeing the ship that Miguel had found.

She assumed he had found it and made the arrangements, else he should be back by now. But she couldn't see much of anything and the fog was starting to roll in from the sea. She started to wonder if she would be able to see the ship even if Miguel got the lights out.

Finally Cordelia just couldn't take the waiting anymore. She cast Wings and headed for the edge of the roof. She slipped on the tiles and started to fall, then her wings swept out and caught the air and she was in flight. She flapped hard, afraid of hitting one of the other buildings and managed to get up a couple of hundred feet. Then she let herself glide southeast, out over the bay.

The ship was moving fairly well now, between the rowers in the ship's boat and the tide. They were heading out of the harbor and it was getting hard to see anything, what with the fog. Miguel decided it was time, so he went to the fantail, where he couldn't be seen by most of the crew and held out the light crystals, then waited. And waited. And nothing much happened. Miguel's arms were getting tired.

"What are you doing?" said a woman's voice from behind him.

Miguel whirled to find a woman who seemed to him to be middle-aged, perhaps thirty. She was wearing a uniform coat that proclaimed her to be an officer of the ship, first or second officer. Her voice when she had spoken, Miguel now realized, had sounded curious, not hostile. "I, ah, I'm signaling a friend." Lying on his feet wasn't a skill that Miguel had, nor one that he wanted.

"And does the captain know about this?" Her voice, while not threatening, was noticeably cooler.

"No. But not for lack of me trying to tell him," Miguel hastened to reassure her. "He said he was busy and we would talk about it later."

She snorted. "That sounds like Rodrigo. So who is this friend you're trying to signal?"

"Cordelia Cooper, a wizard. She is flying out to meet us if she can find us in this soup."

"And why didn't she use the gangplank like normal people? For that matter, if she can fly, what need has she for a ship?"

"Well, she can only fly for a few hours at a time," Miguel explained. "At least I think that's how the somebody's Ethereal Wings spell works. Mostly, what she told me about it was that she wasn't very good at flying. Which, when you use Wings, is something of a skill like swimming. Apparently it doesn't take skill when you use a regular Fly spell, but they don't last as long and they use more magic.

"I don't understand magic. Noron gives me spells but I barely know what they do and how to invoke them. When Cordelia gets to going on about how magic works and the theoretical underpinning of the practice spell, my eyes cross and I want to go take a nap."

Miguel was babbling and he knew it, but at the same time it was working and he knew that, too. Miguel was quite good at appearing harmless and endearing, which made older women like him, but unfortunately made girls his own age despise him. Or worse, want to be friends.

"And why didn't she use the gangplank?"

"Well, she ran into some trouble in Arginia."

"What kind of trouble?"

"Well . . . bad trouble," Miguel said.

The woman's eyebrow went up, she reached out a hand to take his crystals away, then, with a whoosh, Cordelia swooped over their heads and landed up above them, on the poop deck.

The officer's hand descended on Miguel's shoulder and she forcibly turned him around toward the ladder. "Let's go greet your friend, young intercessor."

* * *

Cordelia had been flying around the bay for a while, looking for the lights. She'd seen several ships, all of them heading out of the bay, but she hadn't seen much in the way of lights. There was generally a lamp of some sort on the bowsprit of each ship and often another on the poop deck or aft deck of each ship, but it was hard to tell. She saw a couple of moving lights on a ship and headed that way. As she got closer, they looked like her light crystals, but she couldn't be sure. Then they moved and she couldn't see them anymore. She flew closer to that ship, and saw them again. Yes, that was Miguel, talking to a woman in uniform.

Cordelia's wings were getting tired. That wasn't exactly right, because magical wings didn't get tired the way flesh and blood wings would. But Cordelia wasn't used to flying and, well, it felt like her wings were getting tired. They were supposed to last for seven to nine hours at her level of power, but she had never flown for more than half an hour at a time in her life. Mostly, it had been little practice runs, just to prove to her teachers that they worked and that she could, in fact, get into the air.

Actually, it was Cordelia's body that was getting tired. She had to hold her body in certain ways when flying, and hers wasn't used to it. So she was tired and worried and in a hurry to get her feet firmly on the ground.

As soon as she was sure that it was the right ship, she went in for a landing. She misjudged the speed at which the ship was moving. Not by much, as it wasn't going very fast and looked like it was stationary from any distance. So she came sailing in and suddenly she was too far back and too low. She flapped madly and then she was too high and was about to overshoot. So, she backwinged and landed on the poop deck of a ship that was making a good three knots.

Now, three knots isn't fast. It's less than three and a half miles per hour. You can walk faster than that. But when you land on something that you think is stationary and it's moving at three miles an hour, you land badly.

"*Oooff*," Cordelia said as she repeated her first experience with wings by flapping too hard in the wrong position and landing on her bum.

Ensign Crus was frightened half to death. "A roc!" he shouted as he went over the railing from the poop deck to the quarterdeck. Fortunately, he was an agile lad and did no more than sprain an ankle.

But his shout was enough to bring everyone's attention to the poop deck where by now Cordelia was sitting, trying to decide whether to dismiss her magical wings or fly away.

The helmsman was made of sterner stuff—or at least had a few more years and had actually seen a wizard flying using the wing spell once when he had been at a fair in his youth. So, he held to the wheel and didn't scream. It was a near thing, though in later years he would never admit that. He would, however, tell the story of Ensign Crus' flight over the railing, until it was Captain Crus he was talking about.

By now, Miguel and Second Officer Batuca—who was also Mrs. Butuca, wife of the captain and the purser on the *Maranho* and was actually the person that Miguel should have gone to to see about a passage for Cordelia—had reached the poop deck. Not that that piece of information would have done him any good since she was in the same bed as the captain and the crew were, if anything, even less likely to willingly incur her wrath. Officer Batuca had a sharp tongue and a quick way with slovenly crew.

"I think I'd like to know exactly what is going on," Second Officer Batuca said. "And I'd like to know it right now."

Most of the sailors who heard her flinched.

She pointed at Cordelia, then at Miguel. "My office. Now."

* * *

The purser's office, at least on this ship, was off the captain's cabin. For obvious reasons. It was a pleasant little room, accent on the little, about ten by fifteen feet, with a fold down desk built into one wall. The desk was folded up when they arrived, and Officer Batuca unfolded some chairs for Cordelia and Miguel, then took a seat in what was obviously her own chair.

"All right," the formidable woman said, "Wizard Cooper, please tell me what is going on and why we shouldn't turn this ship around?"

Cordelia was fairly certain that the captain wouldn't do that, but she explained the circumstances of her leaving the city. Then Miguel explained why he hadn't explained them to the captain, and the second officer nodded. "I'll tell you the truth, Intercessor, Wizard. Our crews have run-ins with port constabularies on a regular basis and, as a general rule, we are in no particular hurry to turn people over to them because we are always the strangers, and justice in such places always seems to favor the local over the stranger. So, yes, we'll provide passage, but not free passage. We aren't a charity and you, Wizard, aren't an intercessor who might expect passage on religious grounds. Intercessor, do you happen to have a healing spell? Ensign Crus could probably use some help. Wizard, what do you want? Work your passage or work as crew, or neither of those?"

"That's the question. I could probably pay for passage, within reason, though I am not all that wealthy. And a part of me really wants to, if we can reach an agreement on the price of that passage. We will be going on from the trade enclave in the elven lands, and I will probably need to pay for passage from there."

"Going to where?"

"Pango Island."

"You won't find a ship from Elfsain to Pango. The only ships that dock there are Nasine ships. You will probably have to take passage to the Nasine colony in the Orclands. Ships of all flags, even KOTC ships, dock there."

"Which means all the more cost I will be facing. Still, I am getting very tired of spending so much of my time getting from one place to another." Cordelia stopped and blushed, suddenly realizing that her last comment could well sound like an insult. "Not that that applies to you." Cordelia stopped again. "If you'll give me a moment, Officer Batuca, I'll try to get my feet out of my mouth so I can speak more clearly. I'm a wizard by training and inclination. So time spent getting from one place to another is, for me, time wasted. Time I could be spending making magical items or doing other magical things. I have spells in my books that would let me travel much more quickly, but I haven't had the time or the incentive to focus on learning to use them."

Cordelia was talking about the translocation spell that was in the spell book that she had gotten from the elven cave several years ago.

"I would like to use my time on this trip trying to learn those spells, but I can't afford too much in the way of price of passage, so if it's going to be too expensive, we will have to work out some sort of deal for me to work my passage as crew."

"Oh, you don't want to be crew, Wizard." Officer Batuca raised an eyebrow. "Just what is your wizard rank? You aren't wearing wizard robes. I think we are safe in assuming that you really are a wizard, considering the way you arrived."

"That's not altogether a safe assumption, ma'am. That spell can be cast on others as well as the wizards themselves," Cordelia told her. "In this case, though, I am a Wanderer Wizard. Specifically, I am a silver book wizard and an orange natural wizard."

"Let me guess. You were wearing wizard robes when the man attacked you?"

"Yes."

"I'm not all that fond of elves, but I'm pragmatic about it. It's probably true that elves are more prone to producing natural wizards than humans, but there have been human natural wizards for all of recorded history. The notion that natural wizardry means elven blood is just plain silly. But they believe it in Arginia. So since you were showing two different wizard ranks, they assumed elven blood."

"It probably didn't help that she was wearing an elven cloak and elven boots at the time," Miguel added.

"Probably not," Cordelia agreed, "but that's beside the point, I think. What do you charge for passage to the Nasine trade enclave in the Elflands?"

"Weeelll, that's an interesting question . . ." said Officer Batuca, which started a marathon bargaining session in which Cordelia was convinced that she was not only taken to the cleaners but cleaned, folded, and put away as well. She ended up paying some, though not much, money and doing some, but not that much, work for the ship. Some mending, some flavoring, and a bit of flying about as a scout.

That last was fairly useful for her, as well as for the ship. She got practice using her wings, and though she doubted she would ever be truly graceful in the air, she at least became fairly competent.

She also spent quite a bit of time in her cabin with her spell book out, practicing translocation. She couldn't craft the whole spell, but she could craft parts of it. And she thought she was beginning to understand it well enough that she could probably make a magic item to hold it, so that she could craft it into the magic item.

CHAPTER 8

Location: The Maranho, at Sea, off Amonrai
Date: 15 Justain, 773 AR

"**N**ow tie this around your waist," Wizard Cooper told Ramon. So far this had been the strangest trip of his life. Starting with finding an intercessor sleeping on the deck and then getting really weird.

He tied the rope around his waist, wondering why he had volunteered for this. As part of Cordelia Cooper's agreement, the ship was entitled to at least five hours a day of flying scouting, weather permitting. But Cordelia didn't have to be the one doing the flying. When that had been explained, the captain had asked for volunteers, and Ramon had risen to the challenge.

"When I cast the spell, the wings will appear on your body, folded. Leave them that way! Don't try to extend them until I tell you to."

"All right," Ramon agreed, nervously.

She stepped behind him and touched him twice, once on each shoulder, and he felt the wings appear. It was a very strange feeling, almost like another set of arms but not quite. He wanted to stretch and almost did, but remembering her instructions, kept still.

"Very good," she said, walking back in front of him. "Now, slowly stretch your wings out."

Ramon was facing inboard and did as he was told. Then he felt the pressure of the wind. Ramon was a sailor and knew the feel of the wind, knew almost instinctively what it meant. They were sailing east southeast with the wind from port abeam and they were on the landward tack toward the Panith peninsula. That left the wind blowing in Ramon's face at about three knots. A light breeze.

All that, he had known before stretching out his wings. That sounded so strange even in his own mind. *His wings.* His wings were pushed by the wind, each individual gust, and hard. Though his face and hands were still telling him it was calm, his balance was telling him he was facing gale force winds. He did what he would normally do facing a gale force wind. He hunched over into the wind, leaning forward to maintain his balance. In this case that also changed the angle of his wings. and pressure became lift. Not enough to lift him into the air but enough that he felt considerably lighter on his feet and he was still being pushed pretty good by the breeze.

Curiosity got the better of him and he hopped. Just a bit, but it was enough. He lifted off and the wind, no longer held in check by his feet on the deck, pushed him back until the rope around his waist came taut. The pressure on his body from the wings was above the rope. He flipped backwards. The wings that had been pushing him up were suddenly pushing him down and he landed on his rump with a thump.

The wizard was grinning at him. Not unkindly. "I did exactly the same thing the first time I tried my wings. Well, close enough."

Ramon grinned. After all, this was hardly the first time he'd fallen on his rump. He pulled in his wings, climbed to his feet and tried again.

Location: The Maranho, at Sea, off Amonrai
Date: 18 Justain, 773 AR

"Watch yourself!" Miguel shouted as his short sword flicked out and scored on Ramon Crus.

Ensign Crus gave him a dirty look. "Once more, you villain! You'll never beat me! Never!"

"I see the boys are playing again," Officer Batuca said to Cordelia, who was watching arms practice from a safe distance.

"They're boys. They're always playing."

Play, in this case, was swordsmanship class with Miguel as teacher and the shortish ship's swords as the weapons. As an intercessor of Noron, Miguel was all about trial by combat and that, in turn, meant that he was all about skill with weapons. All sorts of weapons, in all sorts of circumstances.

"I'm surprised to see an intercessor, even an intercessor of Noron, so skilled?" Elena Batuca's voice held the question.

"I picked up the reason for that a little at a time over the last several months," Cordelia said. "He is the youngest of three sons, and you know how Nasine gentry is brought up. Fight at the drop of a hat, defend your honor to the death. Well, his older brothers took that to mean that they needed to teach him to fight. And being the smallest as well as the youngest, he got worked over pretty good. But Miguel is fast."

Elena snorted. "I can see that."

"You can? Honestly, I can't. I'm not a very good fighter, so far as sword work is concerned. It's all too fast for me to follow."

"Oh, he's fast," Elena said. "I grew up watching young men like those in his family, and he's phenomenal. I wasn't of the gentry class, just a sailor's daughter, so my brothers and sisters weren't actually involved. But the gentry were at swordpoint all the time and we learned to recognize who was good. And believe me, that young man could make a living as a professional duelist."

"So I gathered," Cordelia agreed. "Apparently that is what brought him to the priesthood. He did fight a couple of fights that were real, and when he was about fifteen someone approached him to try and get him to challenge someone. He was offered money and that deeply offended his sense of honor. Then his family was threatened and he didn't know what to do or how Noron could allow such things. So he went to his intercessor, who was apparently a decent sort. I know that Miguel speaks of him in glowing terms. The intercessor got him out of the mess and into the temple as an acolyte. From whence he was sent to college in Kronisburg, partly to get him out of the way of the people his lack of hypocrisy had offended."

"That makes it quite a bit more clear."

"Really? What?"

"Noron doesn't normally give spells to those so young. Nor do most of the gods, for that matter. But that kind of skill at that age . . . that's even less common. I was beginning to wonder if he was secretly fifty, except that in most ways he is a typical teenage boy. But mostly it's that intercessors of Noron tend to be pretty full of themselves, whether they get magic from him or not. But this boy isn't. He acts more like he has to live up to the faith people, and especially Noron, have put in him."

✳ ✳ ✳

Riposte, and in across the ribs. Miguel was intentionally moving more slowly than he could but the young ensign was still letting him in. "You can't let me pull your blade out that way, Ramon. If I get it that far out, it lets me through."

"All right. How about this?" Ramon's sword shot out and then pulled back, but just a touch, before darting down to try and get under Miguel's.

Miguel danced back. "When you need room, take it. Step back, step to the side, whatever works and whatever keeps you out of corners where you can't maneuver."

"Sea room," Ramon agreed. "Never let yourself get caught between a pirate and the shore."

"Quite right."

They broke apart and went for towels to dry off. Sailing in the tropics is both hot and humid. Add in exercise, and you get sweat. Lots of it. Off in the distance you could barely see the tip of the Panith peninsula, and there was a freshening breeze starboard abeam. They had been at sea just long enough for everyone to get used to the routine, and the hardest part of the voyage was probably behind them. Now they just had to go with the wind and the current. They wouldn't spend as much time tacking back and forth. At this point, the danger was pirates and the occasional sea monster.

The Gulf of Panith was marginally well patrolled and fairly safe, but the sea lanes along the southern coasts of Amonrai weren't. That was why they wanted someone in the air.

"It's like this, Wizard," Ramon told her, "if we can see them before they can see us, we can avoid them. And it's better to avoid them than run from them."

The wizard nodded and cast Wings on Ramon again. Once she was out of the way, he spread his wings and flapped, just enough to get a little lift. By now they had come up with a harness that he wore for his flight training. It went around his shoulders and waist, and the knot was mid-chest. With a few flaps, he could get a little height and then they let out the line and he slowly got higher and higher. After that he didn't need to flap at all and could control his flight with slight adjustments to his wings. In a few days he would probably be allowed to fly without the tether, something he was really looking forward to. Ramon just couldn't understand why the wizard preferred sitting with her nose in a book to soaring through the heavens, but he was thankful for it. It gave him this once-in-a-lifetime opportunity to learn to fly and to soar through the winds like a bird.

With the line out to three hundred feet, Ramon was a hundred and seventy feet high and looking out over an incredible vista of ocean. He could see the peninsula in the distance and half a dozen ships, either in the gulf or rounding the peninsula like they were. It was glorious. So great, in fact, that it was hard to keep his mind on what he was supposed to be doing. He took note of the position of the ships and looked for clouds and signs of weather. But from this distance, the world moved in slow motion and it would take hours or days to manage a good track.

Ramon stayed up a little longer than he should have, then landed and reported before his next flight. The drawback of the wings was they couldn't be turned off and on. He could fold them up, but they were still awkward and got in the way. If they were dismissed, the only way to get them back was to cast the spell again. Unfortunately, the wizard would only cast it once a day, so Ramon spent a lot of time dealing with the awkwardness.

Location: The Maranho, at Sea, off Amonrai
Date: 25 Justain, 773 AR

Cordelia created in her mind the complex form in scintillating purple and green with specks of gold. The specks, her spell book told her, had to be in just the right place and they kept wanting to move. Cordelia was running into a conflict between the book and the natural wizard in her. The natural wizard wanted the specks here and the book said they went there. There was something wrong and she couldn't figure out what it was.

It would be years before she figured out that both the natural and the book parts of her were right—within workable limits—but the natural was more right if she managed *not* to consider where she was going while she was crafting the spell. Her natural magical sense wanted to put the gold specks at the destination location if she let herself think about it before the spell was cast.

✴ ✴ ✴

Miguel was having quite a good time while Cordelia was working on the translocation spell and Ramon was flying. Like most ships, this one had a mixed crew. But it was still a Nasine ship and the crew was mostly from his homeland. He could speak the Nasine language and expect to be understood, and he was finding that he had missed it while speaking Doichen and Kingdom at college. But it wasn't just the language. The almost Dwarven practicality of the Doichen people could get irritating. So talk of sword play, honor, and adventure was very much a relief for him. Naturally enough, he told of the quest they were on and was quite surprised when the crew was less than thrilled with the fact that Cordelia and her friends had caught a Nasine smuggler.

Location: The Maranho, at Sea, off Amonrai
Date: 26 Justain, 773 AR

The tray wasn't tossed onto the table. The steward was much too well trained for that. But it wasn't delivered with quite the same smoothness as it had been for the first few days of the trip. Nor, Cordelia noted, with the same smoothness that the captain, other officers, or Miguel received. Cordelia was seated at the officer's table in the mess hall. Both she and Miguel were nominally of the officer class on the ship, Miguel because he was an intercessor, and Cordelia because she was a wizard. Even on a freighter like this, where there were only twenty-seven total crew from captain to ship's boy, there was a clear distinction between officer and crewman.

Having spent most of her life on the other side of that divide, Cordelia was not exactly more aware of it than her fellows, but perhaps more aware of the falseness of it than most. She didn't comment on the slight bump as the plate arrived, nor on the fact that her stew was a bit more prone to gristle than it had been in the first few days of the voyage.

Cordelia's position was still rather precarious. Miguel was both an intercessor and a Nasine, but Cordelia was just the strange wizard from Amonrai, and perhaps now that they were less afraid that she would turn them into toads, their resentment of her was surfacing.

* * *

Cordelia never had a notion why the crew cooled to her, but their resentment had pretty much dissipated long before they reached the enclave. Partly that was because Miguel, realizing his mistake, went to some lengths to explain and justify Cordelia's role in the matter. And partly it was because, thanks to the flying lookouts, they spotted several ships that might, or might not, have turned out to be pirates and so avoided them.

It was a friendly crew that they left on arrival at Elfsian Port, the Nasine trading enclave near the wild elven lands in the far western reaches of Amonrai. Elfsian was not a particularly active port. In general, they could expect two or three ships a month, sometimes more. Sometimes Elfsain Port went months without a ship coming into port. The goods traded there were mostly furs, nuts, and elven magic of one sort or another going out, woven cloth, steel, and bronze implements coming in.

While the free elves didn't farm like humans, they did have trees that they took care of. Several of those trees produced fruits and nuts of excellent quality and unique flavors, which were much in demand. It takes a lot of fruit and nuts to feed a tribe of elves, and corn makes for a much richer diet. So there was a small but consistent trade.

CHAPTER 9

Location: Nasine enclave, Elfsain, Amonrai
Date: 18 Prima, 773AR

The day was clear and blue, and the breeze from the bay was warm and fragrant. The trees here were more like those of Good Landing in the Orc Lands than like the pines and oaks of Cordelia's youth or the trees near the university in Doichry. This was a land of bananas and coconuts, mangoes and pineapples. Cordelia looked around and already felt hot. New clothes were definitely in order.

"So what are we doing now?" Miguel asked.

"First, we find a place to stay, then we see about some clothing more appropriate to the climate," Cordelia answered.

They walked along the docks to a dirt road which led up the hill to a small hamlet. The buildings were mostly made of wood, lightly constructed. As they entered the town they could see a river off to the right. It was a decent-sized river, but not huge. And they already knew that on the far side of that river was Elven territory. They were looking for an inn and just the short walk from the pier had left them sweaty.

"That's interesting," Miguel said and pointed to one of the buildings. "See the gap there."

Cordelia looked and realized that there was a gap perhaps a foot tall between the walls and the ceilings. She wondered why.

"That looks like an inn," she said, pointing. And it did, sort of. It was two stories tall, of wood construction and it had the gaps between the walls and the ceilings on both floors. It had a wide wooden porch with rocking chairs which, at the moment, were occupied by an old human and a young-looking elf, who were talking to a much younger boy who appeared to be half-elven. There was a wooden placard that displayed a beer mug over a bed.

They walked up the three steps onto the porch under the watchful eyes of the elf and the human.

"Is this an inn?" Cordelia asked, though she didn't doubt it was.

"Best in Elfsain," the old human said. "Go on in. My boy'll look after you. Alfonso, show them the way."

The half elf rose and motioned them to follow.

The old human's "boy" turned out to be his son, Alberto, who was also Alfonso's father. These days, Alberto was the one who ran the inn.

"It was Papa's before I was born, and back then it was barely a trading post," the middle-aged "boy" said. "I'm Alberto, my father is Carlos. Did you want one room or two?"

"How much for a room?" Cordelia asked.

And that started the negotiations. After a few minutes, Cordelia decided that as much as she would prefer the privacy of her own room, her finances wouldn't support it. She did still have to get herself and Miguel to Pango Island, after all.

While they were negotiating, Alfonso wandered back out to the porch and an elven woman dressed in a diaphanous gown came in. She was short and slight, like most elves, with the golden hair and pointed ears that were common to her race. She walked up to Alberto and kissed him on the cheek, then smiled at Cordelia and Miguel. "As soon as you're finished with

Alberto, I'll show you to your room," she said. Then with a quick gesture, she cast a spell which lifted their bags about a foot off the floor.

When Cordelia and Alberto settled on a price, the elven woman led them to their room, their bags following docilely behind her. "I'm called Galengasi, Harvest Moon in the human tongue," she said. The human tongue she was speaking of was Nasine, which only made sense, since they were in a Nasine trading enclave.

"I'm happy to meet you," Cordelia said. Cordelia wasn't wearing her wizard robes, not wanting to advertise her status at this point. Not so much that her wizardry would be a problem here, but because she was hoping to catch a ship directly to Pango Island and it would be better if that ship's crew didn't know she was a wizard. Cordelia was still quite concerned about the debt that Mrs. Tomson was claiming against her. The problem was that not acknowledging herself to be a wizard cut off her only real source of income. "Are there many wizards in the enclave?" she asked Galengasi.

"Quite a few among the elves," Galengasi answered. "Generally speaking, an elven wizard can get more for magical items here than anywhere else. That draws us. That's what brought my father here."

"Your father?"

"The elf you saw sitting on the porch. Papa and I came here about sixty years ago. I had just come out of a tree and we worked for several years, making magical items and getting to know Carlos and Maria. Then Papa merged with another tree and I was thinking about doing the same thing, but Maria was a friend. Then Maria died and I merged with a tree. When I came out Alberto was just turning into a young man and such a beautiful young man he was—and, well, I decided to stay out for a while."

Location: Nasine enclave, south coast of Amonrai
Date: 24 Prima, 773 AR

From their conversations over the next few days, Cordelia gathered that Galengasi was some three hundred years old, while her father was closer to twelve hundred. They were both natural wizards and neither was particularly powerful. Cordelia asked about book wizardry and learned that they had seen some among the Nasine and had even been shown spell books, but couldn't get their minds around the symbolic representations of what, to them, was a natural thing—as natural as breathing or falling in love.

Which was not to say they weren't skilled. They were, but their skill in magic was the slow kind. They would spend years slowly and carefully adjusting the branch of a tree to just the right shape to make an elven harp or to have a coconut grow in the shape to make a wine container with coconut wine inside.

Cordelia sat looking at a coconut wine bottle and a normal coconut. The husk had been removed from both and the differences were striking. The normal coconut was round like a nut with a rough surface, but the coconut wine bottle had a flat bottom and a neck and a smooth, satiny sheen. The wood of the wine bottle coconut was also much thinner. So thin, in fact, that it was translucent; she could see the wine in the nut. Partly that was because it had been carefully polished, but mostly because it had been encouraged to grow that way by a series of spells cast first on the coconut tree as it grew and later on the coconut itself. Other spells had adjusted its shape and introduced the yeast that caused it to ferment.

It was beautiful, subtle work and Cordelia longed to try the wine just to see and taste the result. But the wine was two reali a bottle, even here. In a restaurant in Kronisburg it would be ten times that and even more in Yorkin. Part of that was simply that the only place that made this particular type of coconut wine was right here. They were grown in Galengasi's coconut grove just a few miles from here and aged in the wine cellar of the inn.

Most of the magic of this trading enclave was like that. Slow, careful, incredibly detailed work. The elven wizards would take months on something that a human would only spend hours on because they expected to keep it for centuries. And that attitude carried over even to things like the coconut wine.

The inn where Cordelia and Miguel were staying was a construct of living trees, hand-worked wood, spiderwebs and handmade knickknacks collected over the years. Even the dust rags that wiped down the oak bar were hand-knitted spider silk.

Very little was rushed or hurried, and what little was, was mostly the human influence.

"This place seems an awful bustle compared to the elven lands across the river," Galengasi told Cordelia, "but I like it. It's so vibrant."

Cordelia raised an eyebrow at that and Galengasi laughed. "It's true," she said. "I have been to other human settlements and I know that to you humans this place seems as stolid as a mountainside, but compared to the true elven lands it is very active. Pure human settlements seem cacophonies of constant change with the new rushing in before one has a chance to see more than a glimpse of the old."

Cordelia looked around the comfortable room, at one of the pylons. The inn was held up by what at first appeared to be twelve round wooden pylons driven into the ground. Closer examination revealed that each of those pylons was in fact a palm tree that had been grown carefully with the structure of their growth adjusted by spells and the inlaying of magic moss.

"They are minor spells," Galengasi explained. "But they take a long time to have an effect and you have to cast them every day. That was the deal that father made with Carlos. Carlos was going to chop down some trees to build the inn and, well, my father was quite fond of that grove. So he made a deal with Carlos that he would guide and speed the tree growth. Well, even with guiding the trees and speeding their growth, it takes years to grow a tree, even a palm tree. But father managed to convince Carlos and Maria. Maria was Carlos' wife. She's gone now." There was a brief flash of bitterness in Galengasi's expression, gone almost before Miguel or Cordelia could see it.

"So my father had to sweeten the deal, if he wanted to save the grove. So they went into business together, with Carlos handling things when Father merged with a tree and with me coming in to help as a favor to Father. At first it was a trading post, not an inn. Father and I had connections among the elves and Carlos had connections with the government. It took about ten years to grow the inn. And by then others had taken over much of the elven trade. So we just stayed with the inn. Father was getting a bit creaky by the time the inn was finished and merged, but I stayed around for a few more years till Maria passed. Then it was my time to merge, and I didn't come out until Alberto was a teenager, and, well . . ."

Cordelia nodded and looked around for something else to talk about. At the level of the floor and the ceiling of the first floor, the trunks had been guided to expand and make flat surfaces to support the additional wood for the floor or ceiling. At the roof, the palms branched out and sprouted broad leaves in a carefully designed pattern that shed the rain. The walls had started out as simple wooden panels, but using magic, those panels had been grown into the supporting pillars and were now at least half alive. Cordelia could see the veins of magic and life in the walls. The gap between the wall and ceiling proved to be less of a gap than Cordelia had first thought it was, for a colony of spiders maintained a screening web which both kept insects out of the inn and fed the spiders. It was all integrated and none of it was the sort of thing that you would notice on first arrival.

"So you married Alberto," Miguel said. "Lucky man."

"By elven custom, yes, though even that wasn't easy," Galengasi said. "The authorities here in the compound don't recognize elven marriage and won't marry us by human law."

"Why not?" Miguel asked.

"Because they claim that any relationship between an elf and a human can be nothing more than a fling. And that elven marriages aren't permanent arrangements, anyway. It is true that elven marriages are often much more complicated than human marriages, since it's possible that one of the elves in the marriage will be merged with a tree for years while the other is active. Elven marriage custom takes that fact into account."

Cordelia was burning with curiosity. "How does it take it into account?"

"Well, that depends on the marriage. In some, the marriage ends when one or the other party merges with the tree and in others it is simply suspended. But it is generally conceded that while one party to a marriage is merged, the other party is free to date or even marry again. Which can cause complications when someone, for some reason, comes out of a merge unexpectedly to find their husband or wife married to someone else. So most elven marriages at least acknowledge the possibility of more than two parties being involved. Humans find that distressing for some reason."

"And the local government uses that as a reason to refuse the rites of marriage and, for that matter, the legal protections that marriage offers to you and Alberto?" Cordelia asked.

"The government of the enclave takes the position that it's up to the gods—that is, the intercessors—and if the intercessors refuse to do the rites, then it's not a marriage."

"That seems a poor interpretation of Barra's marriage rules. She insists that there are obligations to bringing new life into the world and that one must prepare for those obligations. So denying you the opportunity to make those preparations would seem to be in direct conflict with the intent of Barra's injunctions. Nor does it seem particularly just to deny you the same rights that a human couple would enjoy." Miguel shook his head in confusion. "Do you mind if I look into this?"

"Not at all."

Location: Nasine enclave, Elfsain, Amonrai
Date: 25 Prima, 773 AR

"She's an elf," Intercessor Patro said, as though that explained everything.

"I had discovered that fact," Miguel grated. "What I don't see is why it should matter."

"That is because you are young," Intercessor Patro said. "You look at her and see a young woman. But she isn't a young woman. She is over three hundred years old. Even if you don't count the time she spent merged with tree, she is almost two hundred years old. To her, to almost all elves, we are children. What she is doing to Alberto is little different than abusing a child. He can never be more than a momentary pastime for an elf. Even among themselves, elves are hardly ever truly faithful in the way humans are. Fidelity is not in the elven nature. Neither is honor. Which you would know if you had a few more years, my son. I knew Galengasi when I first arrived here and she looked then much as she does now. She was the friend of the mother of the boy she is now sharing a bed with. And in another hundred years, she will be playing her games with another human or an elf or both at once. They do that, you know, the elves. They have multiple lovers with no sense of shame about it."

"So you deny them the rites of marriage. And the legal protections that go with marriage. And in so doing, you deny their son legitimacy under the laws of the enclave. Which also denies him the inheritance of his father's property."

"You speak as though we are the villains here. To give them the rites would be to provide official approval for what she is doing. It is immoral, an affront to the gods."

"How?"

"Elves are not human. They don't have the same gods, they don't have the same souls. And what their dalliance has produced is neither elven nor human. An unnatural creation of lust and debauchery."

Location: Nasine enclave, Elfsain, Amonrai
Date: 28 Prima, 773 AR

Alfonso was looking over the coconut grove when Miguel happened upon him. "Hello, Alfonso. What are you up to?"

"Checking the coconuts," Alfonso said. "They need the adjusting spell cast on them about once a week while they are growing so that we get bottles. Mother puts the fermenting spell on them just before they are ready to be picked. Then we take off the husk and put them in the wine cellar for another three years. The wine matures in the nut and it uses up the air, grandfather says, so that it stops on its own when it's ready. But it is a never-ending process, because coconuts ripen all through the year, even on the same trees. It's not like grape wines, where there is a single harvest season each year."

"Have you ever had any of the coconut wine?" Miguel asked.

"On my birthday," Alfonso said.

"What's it like?"

Alfonso grinned at him. "The first time, when I was twelve, it was awful. I hated it. But last year it was all right. Father says my palate has matured. The wine is this very, very pale blue color, and there's coconut flavor in it, but there's something else. Something . . . it's hard to describe. There's a dryness to it.

"Father says some of these will be my inheritance someday." Alfonso shrugged, clearly not wanting to dispute his father verbally, but having doubts about whether he would inherit. But also, Miguel suspected, he was too young to really think about his father dying.

No, for Alfonso now, it would be a question of how he was treated by the other boys and by the adults around him. Miguel was deeply committed to the notions of honor that he had learned in temple as a boy and one of them was that you don't blame the innocent. And this boy was innocent, even if Intercessor Patro was completely right in every other particular. This lad wasn't at fault and was suffering because of a policy that had been instituted by the temple here.

And that, to Miguel, was not acceptable.

Location: Nasine enclave, Elfsain, Amonrai
Date: 29 Prima, 773 AR

"I will perform the rites," Miguel told them seriously. "It should properly be done by an intercessor of Barra but, none being available, it's perfectly acceptable for any intercessor to perform them and they are legally binding. This will also make Alfonso legitimate in Nasine law, assuming his father acknowledges him." Miguel smiled, having no doubt of that.

"What will the local temple say?" Alberto asked.

"You leave that to me," Miguel said. "When do you want to perform the ceremony?"

"As soon as we can," Galengasi said. "There are some people we'd like to join with us for the celebration and some of them will have to travel a bit. Say next week?"

Location: Nasine enclave, Elfsain, Amonrai
Date: 4 Banth, 773AR

"Do you, Alberto, take Galengasi as your wife to share your life and your wealth, your hopes and your dreams, and to share in the bringing up of your children?"

"I do."

"Do you, Galengasi, take Alberto as your husband to share your life and your wealth, your hopes and dreams, and to share in the bringing up of your children?"

"I do."

"Then, as an intercessor of Noron, I act for Barra in sanctifying your union and offering praise for its fruitful outcome." Miguel took the coil of elven rope and wrapped it about their wrists. "Thus, in the sight of the gods and this company, I bind two into one." Then Miguel added a gesture. The rope glowed with a clear, white light.

"The rope will continue to glow," Miguel said, "as long as you remain wed." He'd had to be fairly careful in the ceremony to respect the elven as well as the human customs of marriage. He wasn't really sure why, but his prayers had left him fairly confident of that. Miguel wasn't anything like sure, but he had a sneaking suspicion that when he had decided to perform the wedding no matter what, that some negotiations between the human and elven pantheons had come into play.

Location: Nasine enclave, Elfsain, Amonrai
Date: 6 Banth, 773AR

"We are being invited to leave," Cordelia told Miguel two days later.

"What?"

"When you managed to glow that rope, the high intercessor of Noron here, that Patro character, wasn't happy. And he has major connections in the government."

"He can't undo what I did," Miguel said, "because I didn't do it. Noron did, or possibly Barra."

"So what?" Cordelia asked. "That doesn't make him like it any better. It probably makes it worse. He wants you gone before you can upset any other apple carts. And that means they want me gone as well. There is a ship in the harbor. One ship. And I have been informed that when it leaves tomorrow, you and I should be on it."

"Where is it going?"

"I asked the governor that very question. He informed me that it didn't matter. As it happens, it's heading for the Nasine territory in the Orclands." Cordelia shrugged. "We can probably get a ship there that will take us to Pango Island, or at least closer to it." Then she smiled. "Don't worry about it, Miguel. I guess it was your turn. I got us forced out of Arginia, so it's only fair that you get us thrown out of Elfsain."

CHAPTER 10

Location: Gray Gull, out of Elfsain
Date: 7 Banth, 773AR

Cordelia cast Mend Wood on the capstan and the small crack disappeared. The captain of the *Gray Gull* was perfectly willing to let them work their passage, rather than pay a fare. She felt she would get a better deal from that than a simple fee. After all, an intercessor who got spells and a Kronigsburg-trained wizard traveling together was something of a rarity.

There wasn't any possibility of hiding who they were. The high intercessor of Elfsain had made sure of that, so working their passage was best for everyone. Things went smoothly for the trip to the Orclands. Cordelia cast her spells and Miguel did his healings, and soon enough they arrived on the east coast of the Orclands, where the Nasine Empire held sway.

Location: Port Halcon, Nasine Orclands
Date: 28 Banth, 773AR

Cordelia and Miguel walked down the gangplank of the *Gray Gull* to a world that Cordelia almost recognized, but was totally unfamiliar to

Miguel. The orcs, with their green fur, were the same as they were in the Kingdom Orclands. The culture was different in a way that was more felt than seen, but was apparent in the very air of the place. The difference was all around them, but Cordelia couldn't put her finger on it.

The first stop was the dock master's office, where Miguel's status as an intercessor of Noron at least kept them from being overly harassed. No, there was nothing scheduled for Pango Island today. They would have to ask at the ships. There were two Kingdom Isles ships that were stopped at the port and one of them, the *Seahorse*, would probably change its flag to the KOTC once it was out of sight of land.

The clerk took down their particulars with a dip pen rather than the typewriter that would have been used at Goodlanding in the KOTC. Their names and ranks were written in a bound book rather than on the cards that would then be filed. It was one of the things that made this place different even as the broad strokes of the place were the same.

They were directed to an inn, and for several days they searched for a ship that would be going to the Spice Islands.

While they were there, Cordelia was required to restrain Miguel, sometimes physically, to keep him from challenging everyone from the royal governor to a local fruit seller, based on their mistreatment of the orcs. They were treated with the same casual brutality here as they were in the KOTC territory. They weren't afforded the opportunity here to join the army or, for that matter, to work in the mines. No, that wasn't it. They worked here as well as there.

But then Cordelia had it. The difference finally broke through the similarity. The orcs weren't actually treated noticeably worse here. And the prejudice against them wasn't noticeably more here than there. But there was a respect for work in the KOTC, especially skilled work, but all work, that was missing here. The KOTC was all about getting the job done. Here it was all about presenting the proper image of gentility of birth. And work didn't fit into that. Work was what orcs were for. Work meant you were a peasant in your bones whatever your position, so work itself was denigrated.

That was the difference.

Location: Port Halcon, Nasine Orclands
Date: 11 Noron, 773 AR

Two weeks after arriving in Port Halcon, they met Captain Georgia Ferguson of the *Fair Trade*, at the Sailor's Rest, a large inn that catered to ship's officers. The *Fair Trade* was flying a Kingdom Isle flag, rather than a KOTC flag, but made no real secret of the fact that she was a KOTC ship. The captain, a large woman in a well-tailored uniform, waved them to a chair in the inn's dining area. Well lit by glows, the room was furnished with heavy orcberry wood tables stained a deep dark brown and polished to a high sheen. The place was spotless and the food was excellent.

"I understand you're looking to sail to Pango," Captain Ferguson said as they sat. "As it happens, I'm going that way."

"Thank you, Captain," Miguel said. Cordelia, in keeping with her assumed role as a wood carver and Miguel's companion, kept silent as Miguel continued. "Noron bless you for your aid to our quest."

"Very nice of Noron, I'm sure," Captain Ferguson said with a grin. "But I am a follower of Cashi, and she would never forgive me if I didn't make the best deal I could." She lifted a stein of good dark orcberry beer and winked at Miguel over it as she drank.

That got the negotiations going. They lasted about a quarter of an hour and proved that the captain was a much better negotiator than Miguel was. Or than Cordelia was, not that Cordelia was part of the negotiations. That would have negated her disguise. But she knew that she would have been almost as outclassed as Miguel was.

Location: Pango Island, Spice Islands
Date: 11 Pago, 773 AR

Again Cordelia and Miguel went down the gangplank to a new land, or at least a land that was new to Miguel. It was familiar—and not in a good way—to Cordelia. The same inn that she'd stayed at before was still there, but they didn't go to it. Too much chance of being recognized. Instead, Cordelia and Miguel, after a quick stop at a clothier for boots, headed out into the bush toward the Tomson Plantation.

Cordelia stood on the path, looking to the left, then to the right, then ahead to the left and muttered, "This wasn't here before. I'm almost sure this wasn't here before."

What "this" was, Miguel was hard pressed to imagine. There were trees and vines and flowers and weeds of all sorts, all mixed together, and none fitting quite properly in a single category. Some of the trees seemed to be made of clinging vines and others looked like they might be really tall grasses. Some of the bushes . . . It was a confusing cacophony of life, and the "paths" that Cordelia was looking at seemed to Miguel to be just other bits of jungle, perhaps a little less dense than those around them, or perhaps not.

After staring at the mess for a few minutes, Cordelia said, "I think it's this way." And they went on.

Finally, after their third night in the bush, they reached the coast and it turned out that Cordelia's guess was wrong. They were on the right side of the island, but not close to the plantation they were seeking. The plantation they were on was also worked by lizardmen. Most of the plantations on Pango were. They were treated better, according to the lizardmen, than the ones on the Tomson plantation, which was about five miles along the coast.

The story of Cordelia's adventures three years ago was a legend on Pango Island, or perhaps a cautionary tale. The caution being "Even if you deal with a human, it doesn't do you any good. As soon as that human goes away, you'll be punished and end up worse off than you were before."

They got the outline of events. After Cordelia left, everything was better on the Tomson plantation for about a year. Then Mrs. Tomson married again, and Master Robert Williams took over the management of the plantation and of Mrs. Williams. It turned out that Mrs. Williams was attracted to cruel men. Or, perhaps, she and the wealth of the plantation attracted them. She'd spent much of that year in the capital of Pango, being wined and dined by the Governor Hopkins and his cronies, one of whom was Mr. Williams, leaving the plantation under the care of Hriss, Cordelia's erstwhile guide. Hriss, for a while, was the manager of the plantation and the whippings had stopped entirely on that plantation. And productivity had gone up.

Then Mrs. Tomson got married and things got really bad. Hriss was arrested and fined for inciting to riot, though there hadn't been any actual riot. And since he couldn't pay the fine the governor assessed, Hriss was turned over to Mr. Williams to pay off the debt as a worker on the plantation. And, of course, they all knew that the debt would never be paid off. A lizardman's debts were never paid off on Pango Island. The humans arranged it that way, and then used the fact that the lizardmen didn't pay off their debts as proof of their lack of competence to manage their own affairs.

"That was half the reason they were so upset by Hriss' management of the plantation," the old lizardman they were talking to added. "The lizardmen's level of debt was going down and they knew it."

"And that was making them look bad in the eyes of Cashi," Miguel added grimly. "I am no great fan of the god of commerce. You know that, Cordelia, but she is, from all my discussions with her intercessors at the university, truly concerned with honesty and the true adherence to contracts. I don't think that she is all that pleased with Mrs. Williams at this point. Whether she did it willingly or was coerced will matter little to Cashi. She had a verbal contract with you, the lizardmen, and the sea elves. She violated the clear intent of that contract."

"But verbal contracts are always superseded by written contracts," the lizardman said. "The humans insist on that."

"In human courts, yes," Miguel said. "Because humans can honestly misremember the content of a verbal contract. But in Cashi's accounting house, all contracts hold equal weight, for Cashi can watch the contract being agreed to by the parties involved. And when needed, look into the minds of the contractors to see if they acted in good faith. I will pray to Noron and ask him to call this matter to Cashi's attention."

Cordelia looked at the young Nasine. She wasn't a student of theology, but she knew that intercessors of Noron weren't prone to ask their god to petition other gods of the pantheon, because Noron wasn't a god who liked asking for favors.

Miguel nodded at her. "Yes, this matters enough. It is not just an affront to Noron, but to Cashi as well."

"What are you talking about?" asked the old lizardman.

Cordelia looked at the old lizardman. His scales were faded with the years in the sun. lizardmen were naturally long lived. Unlike humans or elves, they simply had a natural life span that was measured more in centuries than in decades. This fellow was easily over four hundred years old. And it showed. She waved for Miguel to explain it.

"I am an intercessor who gets spells," Miguel said.

The old lizardman nodded.

Miguel continued. "An intercessor who gets spells has an option for asking favors of gods that other people don't, but it's a fairly risky option, especially in this case.

"I can ask Noron not to give me spells if I am misinterpreting his will. That's a risky thing to do because the gods tend to find it annoying, like a three year old threatening to hold his breath until he gets his way. A fairly common response is for the intercessor to stop getting spells for months, years, or the rest of their lives."

Again the old lizardman nodded his understanding. He was familiar, from long experience, with those with power being capricious in its use. Especially if they were annoyed.

"In this case, it's especially risky though, isn't it?" Cordelia asked.

Miguel shrugged. "Maybe."

"Why?" asked the lizardman, who had much less of an accent than Hriss had.

"Because it's not just Noron I might be annoying by making this request. Cashi might well be offended by an intercessor of Noron telling her her business. And Noron's relationship with another of the major gods is much more important to him than one spoiled intercessor who thinks too much of his own opinions."

On the old lizardman's advice, they camped that night in the jungle near the beach.

The next morning, they woke to find themselves surrounded by KOTC guardsmen.

Location: Pango Town, Pango Island
Date: 15 Pago, 773 AR

Pango Island had one town, also called Pango. It had docks, hotels, and a mostly transient population of up to a couple of thousand, mostly servants. It included the governor's residence, the homes of the assistant governor and several administrative personnel, and the factors for the plantations spread out along the island.

It also had the only KOTC operated jail on the island. It was located in the basement of the government house, one of the few buildings on the island built of stone. It was that jail that Miguel and Cordelia found themselves transported to. The next day, Hriss arrived.

"What are you doing here?" Cordelia asked Hriss.

"They wanted me to say that you agreed to have all the money from the ship go to Mrs. Tomson," Hriss said, hissing on the esses.

"What happened with Mrs. Tomson?" Cordelia asked. "She seemed a reasonable woman, and quite bright."

"Mrs. Williams, now. She likes to be flattered, and Mr. Williams flatters well when he wants to," Hriss said. "He convinced her that you would never be back and she needed the money to take care of her son."

"Where is her son?"

"In fancy boarding school in the Kingdom Isles," Hriss said. "That happened right after they got married.

"Why you come back?"

"I promised you that the money would go to you and the sea elves."

"We not blame you. Even sea elves know, wasn't you."

"How are the sea elves?"

"Not good. Governor very angry. Big part, their hunting ground, given to fishing boats. Been struggling, stealing fishing boat catches." Hriss shook his head sadly.

And they went on talking. Miguel listened and considered and wondered. Miguel wasn't a particularly powerful intercessor in terms of the sort of spells he got. They were all, so far, of the lowest level. Cordelia, on the other hand, was a fairly powerful wizard. Especially, she was a very talented natural wizard, and while in some ways natural magic was less flexible than book or amulet wizardry, in some ways it was more flexible. The Third Hand wasn't actually a spell, in spite of the name. It was simply the embodiment of the natural wizardry talent. A natural wizard could move things by using their will. Mostly it was small, light things, but the more powerful the natural wizard, the bigger the thing, the more force they could apply and the farther away they could be from the thing they moved. Cordelia could move fairly heavy things and from a decent distance.

The cells they were in had ironwood bars and were locked by an ironwood cross bar. The crossbar was about three feet long and two inches in diameter and had a handle perpendicular to its main length. To lock the door, it was shoved across the open side of the door and rotated so that the handle engaged the stops. To unlock it, you simply rotated the bar and pulled it out of the path of the door's opening. Something that couldn't be done from inside the ironwood door. It wasn't complicated or particularly hard. Just out of reach for anyone in the cell.

Assuming that someone wasn't a natural wizard.

What bothered Miguel was why they were in this sort of cell. Surely their captors knew that Cordelia was a natural wizard. *Wait. Maybe they don't.* There was this divide between natural wizards and book wizards. Each despised the other. And their captors had Cordelia's spell books. Those were taken when they were arrested, along with her magical items. So they might think she was as disarmed as Miguel was.

That meant they could get out of the cells, but then what? Miguel knelt and began to pray.

Miguel and Cordelia were in one cell, and Hriss was in another. The government of Pango was fine with having a man and a woman sharing the same cell and the same chamber pot, but not a human and a lizardman. Noron wasn't a prude, but Miguel did find the choice in segregation confusing.

Location: Pango Town, Pango Island
Date: 16 Pago, 773 AR

The next morning Miguel prayed again. He didn't receive any spells, and he wondered why. They spent a boring day. At one point he was taken out of the cell and questioned. He was accused of being a Nasine spy. And it was suggested that if he would just sign a document implicating Cordelia for theft and the Nasine Empire for espionage, he would be treated better and not be executed as a spy.

At other times during the day, both Cordelia and Hriss were taken out, and reported that they were both threatened with harsher punishments if they didn't sign various documents. In Cordelia's case, they wanted her to confirm that she approved of the actions of Mrs. Williams and of the judgment of the claims court. Which indicated to Cordelia that Governor Hopkins was afraid of the results of an inquiry into his actions.

It wasn't so much that the home office back in the Kingdom Isles would disapprove of what he did. More that they would be embarrassed by his getting caught at it.

That evening, Miguel prayed again and he got a spell, a new spell. He didn't know what it did. He just knew its name. It was called Path. Not knowing what else to do, he cast it and a small bead of dim light appeared before his eyes. As he turned, the light went from red when he was facing away from the cell door to green when he was facing the cell door.

"Cordelia," he said quietly, "would you mind unlocking the cell door?"

"Not a good idea, Miguel. We don't know where they have my spell books and we don't know where to go after that, even if we did."

"I have a guide. At least, I think I have a guide," Miguel said.

Cordelia shrugged, and Miguel heard the bar shift and move. Then Cordelia pushed open the door. Miguel went out, and the light stayed in front of him. He turned his head to the right and the light turned red. To the left, it turned green. And as he followed the green, it led him to the next cell, where Hriss was being held. Miguel opened it, and Hriss came out. The light turned red again. Miguel turned his head until it turned green. They were in a short hall and the green light led them to another door, also locked from the outside. From his questioning, Miguel remembered that on the other side of the door was the guardroom. During the day there were two guards in it. Now he didn't know.

Again Cordelia moved the bar, and they opened the door to see a guard asleep at a table. He shifted and Miguel hit him. Hard. He tried to get up and Miguel hit him again, truly annoyed at how difficult it was to knock someone out. It took several more blows before the man finally went down, unconscious. By which time the man's face was bloody with a broken nose and several missing teeth. And Miguel's fists weren't in great shape either. He wished he had the gloves used for practice in the salle.

The light was red again and Miguel, with the hang of it now, turned his head until it turned green. When it was green he was looking at the keychain on the guard's belt. Grabbing the keys, he let the path spell lead him to a case in the corner. This case had an actual lock on it, a heavy thing with a keyhole. He tried all three keys before one worked. In the case was their gear. His sword, Cordelia's pack with the bottomless bag, and Miguel's pack with his bedroll and other gear. Hriss didn't have anything.

Their gear had been gone through, and most of the valuables were missing. No, that wasn't exactly accurate. All the money was gone from both their packs. And a jeweled brooch that was a gift from Miguel's mother when he left for seminary was missing too, but his sword was still in the case as were Cordelia's spell books, though all her magical items were gone. The guards had taken what they could readily use or sell. But an intercessor of Noron's sword wasn't readily salable because it was believed, quite accurately, that such a sword in the hands of anyone not its proper owner would bring bad luck to the wielder.

Again Miguel followed the light. This time it led them to an exit and out into the night. They followed three blocks to the east and a block north, then to a garbage strewn path next to a building on stilts. Miguel followed the light and Cordelia and Hriss followed Miguel under the building to a place where someone had stored some boxes under the house, leaving a hidden place beneath the house.

The light went out.

Miguel looked around. Nothing. No light, and he could really use one because it was an overcast night and it was dark as Backnor's heart under this house.

"Where next?" Cordelia asked.

"I have no idea," Miguel answered. "My light is gone."

Hriss hissed something that sounded frightened or angry.

"I guess we wait here then," Cordelia said calmly enough. "I doubt Noron could have given Miguel a more powerful spell. After all, Miguel only started getting spells a few months ago."

"Besides," Miguel said. "Noron doesn't like having people too dependent on him. He showed us the route out, but I suspect that we are supposed to decide for ourselves what to do next."

Hriss hissed some. Which neither of them understood. Then Hriss said, "Lizardmen gods better. Dragons tell lizardmen what to do."

"They take your freedom."

"They tell us what to do. Whether we do it, up to us."

✳ ✳ ✳

Cordelia used her magic to produce a very dim light and they made a little nest in the blocked off corner of the crawl space under the house. Cordelia went to sleep as Miguel and Hriss debated the value of gods.

Location: Pango Town, Pango Island
Date: 17 Pago, 773AR

Cordelia woke early and went through her spell books, looking for something useful. She did find an illusion spell that she thought would help. It was called Look Past and didn't so much hide as blur and make unnoticeable—well, less likely to be noticed—the things within the area it was cast on. With them already mostly hidden, it might well keep them from being spotted.

She cast it and they spent a long uncomfortable day under the house, while Pango Town was searched. Eventually, the search extended out to the rest of the island and it was assumed that they were hiding somewhere in the jungle.

As the sun set, Cordelia was in need of food, and even more in need of a place to get rid of the food she'd eaten the day before. She slipped away and looked for a place to do her business. That was harder than it seemed, but she managed. When she got back, the debate was on going. It had expanded to what their goal should be.

"We can't stay here," Hriss was saying. "The whole island will be looking for us, and my people will be scared. Even they will betray us."

Miguel started to say something disparaging, and Cordelia interrupted. "Remember the slave market in Amonrai? Their circumstances are different."

"Not that different," Hriss said bitterly. "It was one of my people who told the guards where to find you."

"So I'd guessed." Cordelia laid a hand on the lizardman's arm. "But that just means that you're right. We have to get off this island, all of us. But I am *not* giving up." Then Cordelia stopped and considered. "Maybe we should. Not give up on your people, but on this island. I don't see the governor ever allowing your people to be treated as equals. You need to go somewhere else."

"Where?" Hriss asked.

"I don't know," Cordelia admitted.

"Maybe to the elves?" Miguel asked.

"No, Miguel. The elves don't like orcs because they are a made people. Well, there are other reasons too, but that's the big one. They aren't likely to like the lizardmen any more than they like the orcs."

"You can't know that."

"No," Cordelia agreed with a sad smile much older than her years. "But it's a safe guess, and we can't afford to be wrong. For that matter, I doubt the wood elves of Amonrai would be all that accepting of the sea elves. They too have been changed from what Druisii intended. We need some place that isn't occupied."

"An island?" Miguel asked.

"Yes. See if you can get Noron to help with that. Meanwhile, I'm going to see if I can find us some food."

❋ ❋ ❋

That night Miguel got Path again, and they followed him to the port, where they found a fifteen-foot skiff. It had a single small sail and oars for six, three on a side. The skiff was marked with "Property of the KOTC" stenciled on the gunwale and it was well fitted out. Miguel's Path spell led them right to it, then started to blink.

"It's blinking," Miguel whispered.

"What does that mean?" Cordelia whispered back.

"I don't know. I never heard of this spell before yesterday."

"Get in boat," Hriss hissed. And, following his own advice, he climbed into the skiff and started casting off. Miguel and Cordelia climbed aboard. Then Cordelia remembered the Tug spell, which she'd cast enough to know well, but not nearly enough to have internalized. It was not a spell she had ready, so she would have to craft it before she could use it.

It was the middle of the night, and they couldn't afford a light. "I need to craft the Tug spell."

"Yes!" Miguel said excitedly.

"I need light to read my spell book."

Miguel went to the chest built into the back of the boat and found a blanket. The blanket was tented using Cordelia's head as the tent pole. She used her natural magic to make a light, and began to craft. It was a simple spell, and only took about five minutes to craft. Then she cast it into the bow and the skiff began to move.

And it moved fast. The Tug spell had roughly the strength of four good fresh horses. That meant that it moved a ship quite slowly, but moved a skiff fast enough to produce a wake.

Miguel's spell became active again and for a few minutes they had a direction. Long enough for them to get out of the harbor and around the island. They were, in Hriss' estimation, headed roughly in the direction of the Dragon Lands, but not quite.

The Dragon Lands were the northern half of an island continent. The southern half were the God Lands. The island of Pango was located only a few hundred miles off the east coast of the Dragon Lands, and the skiff was traveling north northwest, in a direction that would narrowly miss the island continent. They had no idea what was there.

The Tug spell would pull the boat for about four hours and they could steer using the tiller, so Cordelia rested. She would craft the spell again when this one ran out. She cast the spell again shortly before dawn, and at dawn Miguel cast Path again, and confirmed that they were going in generally the right direction. The chest in the back of the skiff had fishing gear, several bottles of good wine, crackers in a sealed tin, and jam in a sealed glass jar. They wouldn't starve on the trip, assuming it wasn't too long.

CHAPTER 11

Location: Governor's Residence, Pango Island
Date: 18 Pago, 773AR

G overnor Hopkins was at breakfast when it was reported that his skiff had gone missing. He was buttering a fresh roll when the knock came. "Yes, what is it?" he asked irritably.

"Sir, this morning the harbor watch noticed that your skiff wasn't where it was supposed to be," the captain of the Island Police reported.

Andrew Hopkins was an avid fisherman, and had one of the company skiffs reserved for his personal use. It was also fitted out with the best of everything that the island had to offer in the way of cushions and comforts that a fisherman could desire. Before Cordelia Cooper had shown up on the island, he'd been planning to take it out yesterday for a day of fishing and forgetting about the cares and worries of his job.

And it was a job, a big one. Andrew wasn't a lazy man. He spent his days surrounded by papers and reports and making the sort of decisions that gained or lost millions of crowns. He considered the things like "his" fishing boat, and the kickback he'd received from Tomson on the smuggling operation just part of the benefits of his job. But he was fully aware that an accountant from the home office might not share his view of the matter.

All of which meant that if the stupid girl had been planning to keep the money from taking the Nasine merchant ship, he would have let her have it. But the idiot girl had intended to give it to the sea elves and the snakeheads. And that could lead to real consequences. So he'd done his job and put a stop to it.

And now this.

He couldn't report the skiff stolen because he couldn't afford the investigation into that skiff. It had been officially lost in a storm over a year ago. He still didn't have Cooper's signature on confirmation of the prize court's finding, and the investigation of that court finding would lead right back to his kickback from Tomson. And if she challenged the finding of the prize court, it would lead to just that sort of investigation. She still wouldn't get the money, but he would, at the least, be fired. And, at worst, he might actually go to prison. The KOTC wasn't gentle with those found guilty of financial crimes. It was a religious thing.

Carefully, he set the roll on the plate, and the butter knife next to it. "Wasn't the port being watched?" he asked quietly.

"Yes, sir." The police captain swallowed. "But the conclusion was that they had retreated into the jungle, so the bulk of our force was concentrated there. We did consider the possibility that they might try to slip aboard one of the ships in harbor, but a skiff. . . . Governor, we're a hundred miles from the nearest island. Who's going to try that in a skiff?"

"I would," Andrew Hopkins grated. "If I needed to. And apparently, so would Cordelia Cooper, her Nasine accomplice, and Hriss."

"Yes, sir," the police captain agreed reluctantly. "Our best guess is that they are heading for the mainland or Chufka Island, which is at least due west."

"That's your best guess, is it?

"You think they are heading for Chufka Island, where the dragon Chufka maintains that any boat within three miles of his coast is his to do with as he pleases, and he usually pleases to eat the occupants of said boats? You think that, in spite of the fact that they unerringly headed for the one place they could get a boat that you WEREN'T GUARDING!"

"That or the Dragon Lands. It's not a lot healthier to land in the Dragon Lands than it is to land on Chfuka Island. With all respect, that's the other reason we thought they wouldn't try for a skiff. It's fifteen hundred miles south to get to the God Lands. And either we or a dragon own all the nearby islands. Where can they go where they won't be eaten or recaptured?"

That brought the governor up short. Where could they go? It was possible they would try for the God Lands, but as the guard captain said, that was a long way along a very hostile coastline. He considered the problem, but couldn't find an answer. Then he had a thought. What if they didn't go very far at all? What if they just went around the island to a secluded cove somewhere? "Have the coastline searched. You're looking for my skiff."

Location: Governor's Skiff, at Sea
Date: 18 Pago, 773 AR

Hriss was fairly strong compared to a human and he had a decent natural sense of direction. Being cold-blooded, operating at night was a challenge, but on a bright, sunny day he could go on and on. So he was letting Mistress Cooper and Intercessor Cordoba rest while he rowed. The Tug spell that Mistress Cooper cast last night had faded away, but he was pretty sure he was keeping a good course. Of course, he wasn't going nearly as fast without the Tug spell.

Hriss felt like a failure and worse. He felt like he had betrayed his people into the bargain. He was the one who ran off to be a guide. He was the one who convinced his people to help capture the smuggler, though the truth was that was done mostly by the sea elves. But his people on the plantation had taken part, and almost as important, had failed to warn Master Tomson about the attack, and Master Tomson died. So his people had taken the brunt of the displeasure of the authorities, and after Master Williams had married Mistress Williams, things got worse. Then Mistress Cooper came back and Hester had reported them. He was pretty sure that it was Hester. And he even knew why. His egg mate was not strong willed. She was convinced that any attempt to assert themselves would be met by harsh reprisals, and Hriss couldn't say she was wrong.

Intercessor Cordoba woke and yawned, then asked if he should help with the rowing. Hriss shook his head and continued to row. So the intercessor set about his morning prayers.

He got the Path spell and it shifted their course a little.

Eventually Mistress Cooper woke, crafted and cast Tug, and they moved faster for a few hours.

"Where are we going?" Hriss asked.

Intercessor Cordoba just shrugged and said, "That way," pointing ahead.

Location: Brazla's Territory, Dragon Lands
Date: 18 Pago, 773AR

Brazla was not her name, but it was the name she used when she went among humans. She was feeling a bit hungry and considered asking Cogoak if she could have one of the humans he kept for snacking. No. Cogoak was a greedy bastard and would want too much for it. No, she thought, considering. She wasn't at all hungry for life force.

She was, she thought, in the mood for fish. It wasn't a particularly common appetite, but it did happen. She looked around her home. It was a high desert, about a hundred miles from the coast and it was very different to dragon sight than to human eyes. Magic was rich here. It flowed and swirled, and over the past hundred fifty years since she had claimed this particular chunk of desert from the previous owner, she had improved it. By now, though a mortal couldn't see the complexity of the magic, to a dragon it was a castle of magical energy.

She tweaked the flow a bit, but was still feeling a bit peckish, so she stood, shook out her wings, and slipped into the air. A few flaps and a minor spell, and she was gliding east at a leisurely thirty miles an hour. Mostly by instinct, she scouted the ground below for food, but she couldn't hunt here without incurring the wrath of the holders of these lands. So she flew on, ignoring the desert life.

Twice there were magical warnings issued by the dragons whose lands she flew over, but she assured them that she was just passing through, and neither of them were big enough to challenge her for nothing more than flying over their lands.

$$* \quad * \quad *$$

Seven hours later, she passed over the coast and cast a spell to locate a school of tuna. Nothing. She flew on.

Location: Governor's Skiff, at Sea
Date: 18 Pago, 773 AR

Cordelia looked up at the sky and saw a dragon. A big dragon. And it was heading straight for them. With very little hope at all, she readied a wizard bolt spell. The skiff was fifteen feet long and four feet wide. Wide enough for a man to stand safely if he was careful, and the sea wasn't too heavy. Miguel was standing and drawing his sword. Hriss was bowing his head to the bottom of the boat.

Just as the dragon was getting close, it changed. First, shrinking to the size of a human or a lizardman, then, as it landed, its wings disappeared and it took the form of a lizardman. No, a lizard-woman.

"Your wizard bolt would just irritate me, eggling," she said, and took a seat on the bench across the front of the skiff. She looked at each of them, then said, "Say, you're kinda cute. Stand up, lizardman. Did you bring the humans for me to snack on? That was sweet."

Hriss came up from the bow so that now there were three of them standing. Miguel near the tiller at the back of the boat, Hriss near the center and Cordelia between them. She considered. She could cast wizard bolt sitting down quite as well as she could standing. Besides, the dragon was probably right.

She sat down.

Hriss looked at the dragon, and back at them, then back at the dragon and said, "No, great one. I am the property of Dargatha, and these are my companions."

✱ ✱ ✱

Brazla heard the lizardman and recognized the name, even though it was both incomplete and poorly pronounced. "Dargatha is dead, I am afraid. Well, deadish, anyway."

The life cycle of dragons wasn't the simple life cycle of mortals. As dragons got older, they gradually got bigger and more magical. Eventually, if they weren't killed first, they became completely creatures of the magical realms and their mortal bodies just sort of faded away into nothingness. Dargatha had made that transition when Brazla was still quite a young dragon, centuries ago.

"But you're cute. I may keep you."

* * *

When the dragon in the form of a lizard-woman said that last, she wiggled in a way that Cordelia recognized from her last trip to the island of Pango. It was the lizard-woman equivalent of a "come hither" look, and the lizard-folk weren't overly subtle. She looked at Hriss, and if lizardmen blushed, he'd be blushing, Cordelia was sure.

"Be that as it may, we are not yours to dine on, or use in other ways," Cordelia said.

"You don't appear to be anyones," the dragon said in irritation. "I don't see why I couldn't use you however I want."

"It wouldn't be proper," Hriss insisted with rather more dignity than Cordelia felt was altogether wise.

"What do I care for the propriety of lizardmen?"

With her memory of Hriss from her last trip to the island, Cordelia realized where this was going to go. Hriss was a very proper lizardman. He had a girlfriend, or perhaps she was a fiancee. In either case, he was quite literally not going to betray her to save his life. To, in this case, save all their lives. Brass dragons were not known for taking rejection well. In fact, that was true of dragons in general.

Wait half a moment. This was a big brass dragon and dragons as big as this one weren't interested in sex anymore.

Cordelia looked at Hriss, saw him getting stubborn, and went for a distraction. "I thought that dragons your age weren't interested in sex." It wasn't until she'd said it that it occured to Cordelia that that might not be the most politic thing to say. "Ah, sorry if I spoke out of turn. But my teachers at the University of Kronisburg said that dragons over a hundred feet long rarely had any interest in sex."

"Yes, I remember that class," Miguel agreed, putting his sword away. He sat next to the tiller. "Apparently the instinct is overridden by intellect."

"That is a gross oversimplification. Just what you would expect of a human." The dragon made a sound that was very close to a sniff of disapproval. "Herd animals." She shook her head.

"You're obviously an intercessor. What about you, girl? A lawyer?"

"A book wizard," Cordelia said.

"But you have natural magic. I can smell it on you." The dragon's disapproval was replaced by confusion. "Natural magic and that mechanical stuff that the book and amulet wizards do don't mix."

"I find they mix just fine." Cordelia had been hearing that particular old wive's tale for most of her life, as a wizard, especially from Rojer, her former master who insisted that natural magic users lacked the intellect for book wizardry.

Lizardman faces are stiffer and less mobile than human faces, so lizardmen tend to express more of their feeling through posture and less through facial expression. Because of this, lizardmen tended to have a . . . you might call it a "vocabulary" of postures. And the one the dragon was using now was evocative of great interest. Which let Cordelia step back from her anger enough to realize just how stupid mouthing off to a dragon really was.

"I'm sorry if I was rude. But I have been told that natural wizards aren't smart enough to be book wizards as long as I've had magic. In fact, it was one of the first things that my old teacher Rojer told me."

"I think this Rojer of yours would make a nice dragon snack."

"You're a little late with that thought. Rojer was killed in the Patty Orc caves years ago."

"I normally don't care for orcs much. Well, except for snacks. But in this case I approve. So, tell me about book magic."

And she appeared to be ready to sit there in the fifteen-foot-long, four-foot-wide, flat-bottomed skiff for the next two years while Cordelia explained all she had learned of magic in three years of hard apprenticeship and two years of college.

"Excuse me," Miguel said, politely enough, "but is there some place more comfortable where we could talk? Because in my experiences, when a couple of wizards get to talking, it can take a while."

"I am not a wizard. I am a dragon," the lizard-woman-shaped dragon said. Then taking a posture of amusement, she added, "So it will probably take even longer, since dragons naturally have a much greater understanding of magic." Her posture changed to one of consideration. "Come to think of it, I don't think I've had a conversation about magic in a hundred years or so, and that one involved fireballs."

"Do you have a fireball spell?" Cordelia asked.

"Well, of course. How else could I have been throwing them at that moron?"

What came next was about three long paragraphs of hissing, roaring, and screeching that was apparently the name of the dragon that she was, ah, "discussing" magic with. Another reminder, if Cordelia needed one, that one should always be polite when conversing with dragons.

"Well, in that case," Miguel said, "we probably ought to be chatting somewhere with a bit more shade. And before you get into the structural differences between natural and book magic, perhaps you would take a moment and explain—if you know—why Noron would send us all here to meet in the middle of the ocean."

The posture was now evocative of great offense, as though someone suggested that a mouse was in the soup at a fancy restaurant. "Noron doesn't direct *me* anywhere." The posture became considering. "Did he really send you here to meet me?"

"I think he must have. He gave me a spell called Path, and we followed its direction to get here."

The posture took on a cautious feel, something subtle and, Cordelia was pretty sure, not something the dragon was projecting intentionally. Even dragons could be made a bit nervous by the attention of gods, especially major gods.

"Perhaps you have a point. About the comfortable surroundings, anyway." The dragon reached down and grasped the gunwale with both hands, and for a moment those hands became the claws of a dragon.

And suddenly they were in a different place.

It was a lagoon of crystal clear blue water, with fish swimming about, with a sandy white beach, behind which there was a forest of palm trees. The boat moved until its bow was on the beach, and then the dragon stood and stepped out of the boat, and in an instant became again a hundred-fifty-foot-long brass dragon. It took two steps and curled up in the sand of the wide beach, with her head on her front claws and only about fifteen feet from the beached skiff.

"What is this place?" Hriss asked, hissing his speech rather more than usual.

"Oh, just an island I know. Not mine, not really anyones. Though I think—" She lifted a hind claw and scratched the back of an eye ridge in thought. "—that it's in territory that the Nasine Empire claims. Silly human notions. My land is a really beautiful part of the high desert in the Dragon Lands. The magic flow is scintillating, unlike this place.

"Now! Tell me about book magic."

Cordelia tried, but it proved quite difficult. Dragon brains aren't structured like human brains. Their thoughts and the way they approach things aren't like those of humans either. Their eyes are different, seeing different colors, and so the shapes and structures in the spell book didn't translate. It was clear within fifteen minutes that the dragon, who finally introduced herself as Brazla, was going to have to develop her own spell book from scratch and wouldn't be able to use Cordelia's.

Meanwhile, Hriss and Miguel wandered off.

* * *

Hriss looked at the palm. It was very similar to a nut palm that he knew from Pango Island. "Help me up," he demanded.

Shrugging, Miguel gave him a hand.

Using his claws, Hriss climbed the palm up to the bunch of nuts. He tapped them and selected the ripe ones and pulled them loose, dropping them to the sandy soil.

Regretting the necessity, Miguel used his sword to chop off the top of the coconuts, giving them food and drink. And that wasn't the only food and drink on the island. There were any number of reptiles and flightless birds about the size of a chicken. Hriss recognized several plants and could tell that the island would support the food crops that his people preferred. After "dinner" they walked along the beach for over a mile before giving it up and going back.

As they were walking back an idea began to form in the back of Miguel's mind. It was a combination of things. This was such a pleasant place. A nice place to live. His family would love to live here, at least for a time. A house over there amongst those trees, and a little pier where his father could sit and fish. Not that they would ever come here. They were happy at home in Nasine. But this was a lovely place. He looked over at the lizardman.

Hriss was looking at the place like he'd found paradise. And who could blame him. Miguel began to wonder just how big the island was. How many people, how many lizardmen could it maintain.

Then there was Miguel's status. The intercessors were powerful in the Nasine Empire, more powerful than they should be, some said. They could make judgments and unless those judgments were challenged, they stood as law. And they could claim lands if those lands were unclaimed, with the sole restriction being that they couldn't claim them for themselves. In theory, they couldn't profit from making such a claim. Not that that had prevented an intercessor of Noron from claiming all the Orclands for the king of Nasine four hundred years ago and receiving a great reward from the crown for doing so.

* * *

By the time Miguel and Hriss got back to the boat, the sun had set and Cordelia was getting cold and hungry.

"My goodness," Brazla blurted. "The whole reason I was out there over the ocean was because I was feeling a little peckish and was in the mood for fish." She closed her eyes for a moment, then opened them, and said in her dragon voice, "Back in a bit." Then, spraying them all with sand, she flew off.

Cordelia, Miguel, and Hriss set about making camp. There were the coconuts, and Hriss killed a bird with a thrown rock, which they set about cooking over a driftwood fire on the beach.

It was almost an hour later when Brazla returned and dropped part of a large tuna near their campfire. It was just a bit of the tail, but there had to be thirty pounds of tuna meat in it.

Miguel wasn't thrilled about taking the dragon's leavings, but he didn't make an issue of it. He had some questions to ask Brazla and didn't want her annoyed. Hriss thanked her politely and proceeded to cut the tuna into steaks.

CHAPTER 12

Location: Unnamed Island
Date: 19 Pago, 773AR

The sun rose to find Brazla reading over Cordelia's spell book, trying to understand how visualizing those shapes could affect the magic in the way that they clearly did.

She watched as Cordelia crafted her spells and couldn't make heads or tails of how it was working.

There was a polite cough, and Brazla rotated one eye so that she was looking at the intercessor.

"I want to confirm something you said yesterday, if I may. You said you don't own this island."

"No, of course not. The magic flow is all wrong for a dragon's place."

"And no one else does. There isn't a tribe of orcs or ogres that live here? No human kingdom has a colony on the other side of the island?"

"No. As I said yesterday, the island is in a part of the ocean that the Nasine crown claims, but no human or humanoid of any sort other than you three has set foot on this island in . . ." Brazla paused and just sat there for fifteen minutes.

Twice Miguel started to question her. The first time Hriss waved him back, and the second he stopped himself. This was something that Cordelia had never seen, but had heard about. The dragon wasn't actually here anymore, but was in the magic realms. Dragons didn't live entirely in the mortal world, and the older they got the less in the real world they stayed. Though her body was here right now, her "self" was elsewhere. Finally, she came back.

"No, no humanoid of any sort has ever been here and, more importantly, though dragons have visited the island, no dragon or other magical creature has ever claimed it. Why?"

Miguel, who had sat on the beach while waiting for Brazla to get back, stood, bowed, and then formally drew his sword and planted the tip in the sand of the island, then said, "Under the laws of the Nasine Empire, by the power and duties invested in me by the laws of Noron's church, I do claim this island and these reefs for the lizardmen and sea elves of Pango Island for their part in enforcing the—" Miguel's voice took on a sardonic, perhaps even a disgusted tone. "—laws of the KOTC, and in recompense for their mistreatment by that organization."

Cordelia looked at Brazla. In spite of what the dragon said, she was afraid that Brazla wouldn't approve of the humans claiming her island.

Slowly, the dragon lifted its head and nodded to Miguel. "A serviceable oath. Not truly elegant, but you're human after all. Allowances have to be made. I witness your oath before Noron." Then she lifted her head and gave a brassy roar, complete with flame reaching a hundred feet into the sky.

Resting her great head on her front paw, rather like a satisfied cat, she continued. "The dragons know of your claim now. That, of course, doesn't guarantee that they will recognize it. What are human laws to a dragon? But they know of it. Now, how do you plan to get them here when it's 847 nautical miles from Pango to here? That's a long swim even for a sea elf, much less a lizard man."

"I haven't the least idea," Miguel admitted.

"And how are we going to convince them after the disaster that I led them into last time?" Cordelia asked. "I don't see them following me. Or you, Hriss."

"That's an issue," Hriss agreed, hissing a lot on "issue."

Location: Lizardfolk Island
Date: 21 Pago, 773 AR

After spending a day on the island talking about magic, Brazla the dragon flew off. Cordelia, Miguel, and Hriss spent another day making plans, then loaded up the skiff with food. Taking direction from Miguel's Path spell, they headed back to Pango Island and set off. It took them a week, and they were quite low on food by the time they sighted Pango Island. Fortunately, they only hit one small storm, and only the edge of that. But it wasn't a fun voyage.

By the time they got to Pango Island, it was clear that the "we'll take them a few at a time on the skiff" idea wasn't going to work. They slipped into a secluded cove and Hriss went to talk with the lizardfolk.

Location: Pango Island
Date: 28 Pago, 773 AR

After Hriss left, Louanomannian, the leader of the sea elves, showed up. The sea elves had seen the skiff arriving.

"Returning to the scene of your crime?" he asked bitterly. "Irela was whipped within an inch of her life and we can't put her in the coral."

"Why not?"

"There is a mark in the coral where one of us enters it, and if the coral is broken, then we die. There are a few hidden places, but they are occupied and the fishermen are dragging anchors along the coral to damage it. We are a dying people because of you and your plans."

"The injustice wasn't hers," Miguel said. "It was the actions of others. Cordelia acted in good faith."

"And where is the money you gained from the seizure of the ship?"

"In the coffers of the lawyers and Mrs. Amelia Tomson, who is now Mrs. Amelia Williams," Cordelia said. "I got a letter telling me that I was in debt, and all the prize money was spent. That's why I'm here."

"And what fantastic plan do you have this time?"

"Not me. Miguel. He's claimed an island for you and the lizardfolk. It's nine hundred miles away and no one but a dragon friend of ours knows where it is. It has coral. We sailed around the island and it's completely surrounded by coral reefs. The question we don't have an answer to is: can your people use that coral, or only this coral?"

"And I still don't know the answer to the question."

"Then I would suggest that now is a really good time to find out," Miguel said.

Cordelia was feeling too guilty over her part in the sea elves' troubles to say much of anything.

* * *

Irela groaned, trying to find a comfortable place. Sea elves were truly amphibious in nature, as at home on land as in the sea, and also the reverse. She had a room in the house, a leftover from her time as a tutor to Billy. But the room was now a prison, for with her back opened and no coral to rest in, to go into the sea now would be to court the sort of infection that would kill her in a week or less. She might well die anyway. Master Williams was hoping that she would, though Mistress Williams had begged that she be spared, in memory of her service to the family and because she didn't want to have to tell Billy that Irela, the immortal sea elf that taught him about the sea, was dead at his mother and stepfather's hands.

It was Billy's pleading for the sea elves, and to a lesser extent, the lizardfolk that had gotten him shipped off to school in the Kingdom Isles.

Irela shifted, trying to find a comfortable place, and there was a scratching at the wooden slats over the window. Painfully, she sat up and moved the latch. She cracked open the shutter to see Louanomannian.

"I may have found you a coral patch to sleep in," he said.

Irela considered, but not for long. There was no longer anything here for her. Painfully, biting her lip to keep from screaming, she climbed through the window as her back and legs screamed in agony from the whipping she had received.

It wasn't until they were into the woods that Louanomannian told her it was that Cooper human who had found the coral and it was nine hundred miles away. She almost turned around when she heard that. Would have, except that there was nothing to turn around for.

✳ ✳ ✳

Cordelia was waiting by the skiff with Miguel when Lou brought his sister to the beach. Hriss had slipped into the jungle and was going to contact his people and tell them that their dragon, the one that made them, wasn't coming back, for the lizardfolk treated that dragon with religious deference and its commands as holy writ.

Lou's sister was limping and some of the wounds where the whip had cut her had reopened. Elves don't have particularly tough hides and this one was clearly badly hurt. Miguel took a look at her and used his very limited magic for healing.

"Oh, well," Cordelia muttered to herself, "we know the basic direction anyway." But she hadn't reckoned with elven hearing.

"My sister is hurt," Lou said angrily, if quietly.

"I know that. I'm just trying to get her to a place where she can be healed, not just treated. Miguel is a good kid, but he's still a very young intercessor."

Now everyone was looking at her like she was a monster. Cordelia sighed and waved them into the boat. Once everyone was in the skiff, she pushed it out into the creek and got it turned around. Then she cast Tug on the bow, and they were off.

Miguel was still at the stage where he got one spell a day, and that not a very strong one. But, being an intercessor, he got the right spell most of the time, unlike wizards, who had to figure out what to craft for themselves.

They spent the next four hours being pulled along by the Tug spell at a good clip, heading in the right general direction. During that time, Cordelia crafted Tug again. The spell was powerful, but not complicated, so it didn't take all that long to craft.

They passed the first day that way, with Cordelia crafting and casting Tug six times and resting in between, while Lou and Miguel took care of Irela, and occasionally gave her dirty looks because of her uncaring attitude.

It wasn't that Cordelia didn't care, but she had a pragmatic turn of mind, and wanted to get to Lizardfolk Island as soon as they could, so that they could get Irela into the coral, assuming it worked. They still didn't know if other coral reefs would work to heal the sea elves. And if it didn't, the whole plan to free the elves went right into the chamber pot.

And worry made Cordelia grouchy.

The next morning, Noron apparently agreed with her, because instead of a healing spell Miguel got Path and changed their course a bit. Not much, but if they'd stayed on the one they were on, they would have missed Lizardfolk Island altogether.

Location: Pango Island
Date: 29 Pago, 773 AR

Hriss was glad that Cordelia and Miguel weren't going to be here for this, because this wasn't going to be easy. He slipped into the slave quarters of a spice plantation half a mile inland from the one where he was laid and hatched.

Hriss had known the people of that plantation since he was a child and he trusted them. Right now, he trusted them more than he trusted his own egg siblings.

"Hissess," he said. It was a lizardfolk greeting. The lizardfolk had their own language and they spoke it almost from birth. And, unlike in human speech, Hriss was exceedingly fluent in it. He called over a friend and told her what was going on. He asked her for the news and learned that Governor Hopkins was in a panic because they hadn't found the skiff anywhere on the island and had searched every inch of the coast. By now the governor was afraid that they had gone somewhere else.

"They are threatening everyone, and promising that you will be caught. They say that anyone who helps you will be punished. They said you had gone off and been eaten by a dragon." She made a gesture of reverence, for to be eaten by a dragon—well, by their proper dragon—was the best of deaths. The people knew that the only dragon that would eat their people was their dragon, for it was an old and powerful dragon, respected by its fellow dragons.

"We knew that you wouldn't be eaten by any but our dragon."

"Our dragon is gone, Hrossa," Hriss blurted it out. "I was told by the dragon Brazla, and I don't think she lied."

"You know that dragons can lie, Hriss. If our dragon was gone, she would have eaten you and your companions."

Hriss blushed. "Food wasn't what she wanted when she landed on our skiff in the form of a lizard-woman."

"You didn't!" Hrossa said, sounding at least as intrigued as outraged.

"No, I didn't. I am promised," Hriss insisted. "Fortunately, Cordelia managed to distract the dragon Brazla with a discussion of magic."

He told her of their trip to the island and of Miguel claiming the island for them and the sea elves, and Brazla witnessing the claim.

"What does that mean?"

"I asked Miguel about that, and he explained. It is the basis of the Nasine claim to the Orclands and was the basis of their claim to southern Amonrai as well. It means that we own the island by the laws of the Nasine Empire. And, to an extent, the Nasine Empire will defend our claim."

"To what extent?" Hrossa asked suspiciously.

"I asked the same thing. And the answer is 'not to a very great extent.' At least not if we don't have anything of value to trade with them. But the island is off the normal sea routes and would be hard to find without knowing where it is, so we will have time to develop products to trade with them."

"Are you still harping on that notion? My friend, the humans of the KOTC have corrupted you. 'Everything is about money.' Well, it's not. There is family, and the sun, and growing plants. Making things and talking. Money isn't so important."

"It *is* that important," Hriss said. "I'm not saying that it should be, just that it is. Because it is important to the humans. Mostly to those of the KOTC, but still important to the Nasine. It's the key to our chains, what keeps them locked around our legs, and the only thing that will remove them. That is why the governor was so insistent that we not get any." Hriss, in his own language and among his own people, was a persuasive speaker.

142

He convinced Hrossa that there was a chance, and slipped back into the jungle.

Over the next two weeks, he visited a dozen plantations around the island of Pango and, inevitably, word that he was back on the island got back to the humans.

Location: Lizardfolk Island
Date: 5 Wovoro, 773 AR

The skiff reached the breakwater, a strip of coral reefs that surrounded the island with few gaps. The skiff's draft was only inches, so it passed over with little trouble. At low tide, though, the reef would block even the skiff in most places around the island.

They passed over the reef into the calm water beyond it, and Lou and Irela went over the side to swim in the bay.

* * *

Irela was in bad shape. The human girl had been right. Miguel's spells hadn't even kept up with the damage the infected wounds were causing, just slowed the process of her decline. At this point, she could barely swim. Louanomannian guided her to a crevice in the reef.

A coral reef is not a single organism like a tree. It's a complex of life, a whole ecosystem, but that was what the sea elves were adapted to. Irela flowed into that ecosystem and became, for a time, one with the reef. She lived with the reef and, in one sense, being in a reef was better than being in a tree. For as part of the reef she felt the whole reef. She knew what the reef knew, and that was a lot. Much of that knowledge, much of that awareness, would fade when she was healed, but she had it now. She felt the sea, saw the bay and the surrounding sea through a thousand eyes.

This would be a good place for her people. She felt much better about Cordelia now.

* * *

Lou surfaced. "She is in the reef. We won't know for sure how well it works until she comes out, but so far it looks good." He waved at the island. "Let's go in and see this island."

They did. Lou took his trident and went fishing while Miguel and Cordelia made a fire and gathered fruit and other edibles.

They were having a dinner of crab and coconuts with mangos when the dragon sailed down from the sky. It was Brazla, and she wanted to chat about magic.

"Have you considered going to the University of Drakan?" Cordelia asked.

"That wouldn't be a good idea. The dragon I had the argument with is the chancellor, or dean, or whatever of the University of Drakan. We don't get along. But maybe I should try the University of Kronisburg."

That, to put it mildly, didn't strike Cordelia as a good idea. *A dragon landing on the roof of the chancellery building.* Cordelia shuddered.

"I could take human form." Brazla seemed to read Cordelia's mind.

"You would still need money. The registration fee," Cordelia insisted.

"And some form of introduction," Miguel added. "They don't take just anyone, you know."

Apparently Miguel wasn't any more enamored of the notion than Cordelia was. It wasn't that Cordelia disliked the dragon. She actually sort of liked her, now that she was used to her. But dragons, as charming and friendly as they can be when they choose, are dragons. They aren't, as Brazla put it, herd animals or pack animals. They are laid and abandoned to live or die on their own, and most of them die. They are simply dangerous animals until they get to be seventy or eighty feet long, at the age of a hundred or so. And while they can learn to act social, at their core they remain solitary animals, mostly unconcerned with the welfare of other creatures, even other dragons.

"You don't want me to go?" Brazla said more than asked.

"I think it's an excellent idea," Lou said, after swallowing a piece of crab meat. "Cordelia is only learning magic and Brazla needs expert instruction. Besides, Cordelia isn't a teacher. Just because someone can spear a bluefin doesn't mean they can teach someone to hunt. No offense intended, Cordelia, but Brazla's difficulty might be because you're not a great instructor."

Well, of course Lou thought it was a good idea. It would take Brazla to the other side of the world. But Cordelia couldn't say that.

"Well, that's settled then," Brazla said with a big dragon grin. Then the dragon lost its firmness of line and seemed to be almost a cloud of brass smoke. The smoke contracted until it was the form of a human, then the sharpness came back and before them stood a woman. She was a full six feet tall, with an elve's pointed ears and hair the color of spun brass, and even a brass tint to her skin. All of which was showing at the moment because dragons don't wear clothing and Brazla hadn't felt any need to cater to silly human customs.

Miguel looked away, but Lou examined her with an approving eye. Lou was young to be a leader of the sea elves, but he was still over three hundred years old and over half that out of the coral. So he was of a height with Brazla's elven, no, sea elven form.

That form suddenly bothered Cordelia, as she saw the way Lou was looking at it. "Put some clothes on. If you're going to act human, you're going to have to do a better job than running around naked."

Brazla gave her a look, then gave Lou a look. Then she grinned and reached into the air and pulled a dress of brass scales from the air and put it on, not trying to hide herself while she did it. The brass scales were small and diamond or leaf shaped and overlapped, but shifted as Brazla moved, and in doing so seemed to emphasize her very female form.

Cordelia was convinced that Brazla was doing it on purpose.

"No, it's not settled," Cordelia insisted. "I haven't agreed to be your introduction. And I can't leave here yet. We've still got to get the lizardfolk and the sea elves to this island."

"Why?"

"Because I promised," Cordelia said.

Miguel, who was again looking at them but still blushing, added, "We are on a quest to fulfill Cordelia's obligations to the sea elves and the lizardfolk."

Lou nodded his agreement. Then he smiled. "So, I guess if you want to go to this school and learn magic, you need to help us get settled on the island. It's rather a long swim even for my folk. We need a ship of some sort, so unless you can reach into wherever you got the dress and pull out a three masted schooner, we are going to need to take one and that didn't work out so well last time. Or we need to buy one, and I don't have twenty thousand KOTC pounds on me.

"Hriss was right about that. Money matters in dealing with humans. It even matters in dealing with elves, though we handle it differently."

"All right. You've made your point, but I still don't see that it's my problem," Brazla said

"It's not," Cordelia agreed.

"But until her problem gets solved, she won't be in a position to help solve your problem," Miguel pointed out.

"What about you?" Brazla asked, blinking at Miguel with eyes that had eyelashes which seemed to Cordelia altogether too long and thick.

"I'm on the same quest as Cordelia, and Noron has approved it."

"Welllll," Brazla said, stretching out the word, "I guess I could provide the money to hire a ship. But, in exchange, how about the occasional lizardman or sea elf snack? Not all that often. Every year or so."

And suddenly all of Cordelia's comfort was gone. And she *had* been comfortable. Resenting the dragon's looks, disliking the way she was flirting with Lou was a very comfortable human sort of resentment that ignored the fact that a dragon wasn't a human. That a dragon eating a human wasn't all that different from a lion eating a wolf, or a wolf eating an elk. Or, for that matter, a human eating a pig or a dolphin. Dragons were apex predators, as some of her professors liked to call humans. Hriss' people and the sea elves had been bred, or at least changed, so that they would be available as meals, like a farmer stocking a fish pond with trout.

This sometimes charming woman in front of her really did think of her as an occasionally entertaining snack.

"Welllll," Lou drew out the word just like she had. Then he snapped off, "No! I guess we'll just have to use the skiff. Shouldn't take more than three, well, maybe four years."

"I think you're very stingy," Brazla said with a little pout. Then she grinned. "As I would be. Assuming I ever put myself in a situation to need such help."

Then she looked at Cordelia, then at Miguel. And she really looked at Miguel as though she was looking right through him. As though she was considering whether to turn back into a dragon and eat him right here and now. And she spoke to him, but not in Nasine or Kingdom. She spoke Dragon.

And somehow—Cordelia didn't know how she understood. What Brazla said was "My hoard is *mine*. To spend or keep as I see fit. If I do this, you are going to owe me a favor."

Miguel looked shocked, then started to speak, but Brazla interrupted. "Not you, human. Just know, Noron, when the time comes, you owe me."

Cordelia didn't know then or later what the favor was. Just that it had little to do with humans. Or, she guessed, anything mortal.

* * *

Lizardfolk Island was located in the southern edge of the doldrums, and almost a thousand miles from the largest land mass, which was why it was well off all the trade routes. That made it quite an inconvenient location in terms of having nearby places where you could rent a ship. The nearest Nasine port was a trip of over fifteen hundred miles and that port was on the northern coast of the Dragon Lands. It was a trading enclave that the dragons allowed because sometimes dragons liked to buy things. All sorts of things, which mostly disappeared into the dragons' hoards and were never seen again. It was one of two such ports. One was part of the Nasine Empire, the other owned by the KOTC.

Fortunately, it was Bellamy, the one owned by the KOTC, that housed the University of Drakar. Bonito, the one owned by Nasine, was much smaller and was almost as much a pirate port as an official Nasine port. They both had iffy reputations among humans, and even around dragons. Neither was owned by a dragon and neither was the sort of place that a dragon would want. That had more to do with the way the magic did or didn't flow than anything about the land or plant and animal life. As it happened, both were coves that opened into fairly major rivers that went inland.

Which still left the question of getting there.

"I will arrange that," Brazla said. She took Lou's arm in one hand and Miguel's in the other, and was gone.

She was gone for the better part of two hours, long enough for Cordelia to get seriously worried. Then she was back.

"What took you so long?"

"We stopped off for a drink," Brazla said, then laughed at Cordelia's expression. "Think, girl. You took a Nasine merchantman. We had to establish that you and Lou weren't wanted. That took me and Miguel dealing with the chief magistrates of Bonita, Miguel for the Nasine royal governor, and me to deal with the dragon who is acting as the dragon council's representative this decade. And here is your token." She held out a small token made of the scale of a dragon, carved and inlaid with gold, amber, and magic moss.

Then she took Cordelia's arm and suddenly they were in a different place. They were on a cobbled street with street lamps of magical glows, but only about half as many as the street needed, and the street was, as best she could tell, clean. The building they were next to was of stone shaped by magic and Cordelia could see the remnants of the spell. It was done by a dragon, she thought, and some time ago, but not with any great care.

"This way," Brazla said, and led them in through the door.

The proprietor, a stout middle-aged woman, came up and gave Brazla a bow. She said a word that was in Dragon, and waved for them to follow.

She led them to a table in a corner where Miguel and Lou were seated, with mugs and bowls before them. Miguel waved at the bench across the table.

Cordelia and Brazla sat, and more bowls and mugs were brought. Cordelia looked into the bowl. There was a pale brown, lumpy stew of some sort. She took a sip of ale. It was ale, but that was about all you could say for it. She took a bite of the stew. It was beef, she thought, but couldn't be sure. Maybe other things. Whatever it was, it wasn't a patch on the crab from Lizardfolk Island.

She put the spoon back in the stew and left it there.

"What has Brazla told you?" Miguel asked.

She told him.

"Well, aside from our having an expensive room in this fine establishment, that's all that's been done. It's late, later for us than here, but still late enough so that we're unlikely to find anything tonight."

Cordelia nodded. "I wonder how Hriss is doing."

CHAPTER 13

Location: Pango Island
Date: 5 Wovoro, 773AR

Hriss ran through the jungle and heard the sound of hounds behind him. Recruiting had been going well. Perhaps a bit too well. Clearly someone had talked. He went into the stream and headed downstream. They would expect him to cross or go upstream. It might buy a few minutes, but after that, he didn't know.

Lizardfolk were actually quite at home in the water. Hriss waded downstream for five minutes, dove under the deafening stream, and kept going. Water blocked scent, being under water washed it away, at least for a little while. A few quick strokes, and he went back to wading as his skin dried. He kept going. He didn't think staying in the water was a good idea, but he was fresh out of good ideas at the moment. So he trudged on.

It was ten minutes later that he was met by a sea elf. It was one of Lou's friends and Hriss had known him for years. "Is it true? Did you get Irela out?"

"Yes," Hriss hissed. He wasn't at his best. Lizardfolk don't have the internal temperature control that humans do. They don't shiver. They just slow down and get a little dopy. The water wasn't all that cold, but it was night, and the water evaporating off his skin had chilled him.

"Where is she?"

"In coral by now," Hriss got out. "I think I'm cold."

"Yep. I'd say you are. Not going to get any sense out of you until you're warmed up. Come on. Keep your nose out of the water. I'll tow you."

Sea elves, equipped as they were with webbed fingers and toes, swim really well. So well that even in water only three feet deep, they swim faster than they could wade.

The world got a bit vague then, for a while, as Hriss was taken out to the reef and hidden in a nook.

Location: Pango Island
Date: 6 Wovoro, 773 AR

The sun warmed the water he was in, and Hriss came to himself to find Dunnomian staring at him. "Where's Irela?"

"Should be in the coral by now."

"What coral? Where?"

"Island in doldrums, off shipping lanes. Good size. Surrounded by coral reefs. Miguel claimed it for our people."

"You still going to make us all rich, are you, Hriss?" Dunnomian said bitterly. "Didn't you and that human female do enough last time?"

Dunnomian was one of the elves that took the Nasine smuggler and wasn't happy with how things had worked out.

With the sun warming the shallow pool of water, Hriss was warming up fast. "I know you don't trust me, but I have been to the island. I was there when Intercessor Miguel claimed the island for our peoples. Specifically, for both our peoples."

"What does that mean?" Dunnomian was starting to get interested in spite of himself. The sea elves of Pango Island were used to lizardfolk, and comfortable with the way lizardfolk spoke. They, unlike humans, didn't assume that it meant the lizardfolk were stupid so, to Dunnomian, Hriss' speech had just an accent, not a deformity. So Hriss was almost as persuasive with Dunnomian as he would be with another lizard person.

"Nasine law. Important Nasine law. Law that says Nasine own Orclands. Intercessors can claim land, but not for self. Only for others." Hriss explained that the structure of Nasine law was based on contests judged by Noron, the god of contests, and that an intercessor of Noron, especially one who got spells, could make judgments in Noron's name, and if they kept getting spells, Noron was assumed to be in agreement with the judgment.

"Yes, I get that. But we aren't in the Nasine Empire. Our island is claimed by the KOTC."

"Not new island. Not Lizardfolk Island and Seafolk Reefs."

"Seafolk Reefs?"

"Miguel didn't name island or reefs. He just claimed for lizardfolk and sea elves of Pango Island. I named Lizardfolk Island. You name the reefs whatever you want. But, by Nasine law, both island and reefs owned by us. Not just lizard folk or just sea elves, both."

"And Irela?"

"Lou, Miguel, and Cordelia took her to our island. They think those reefs will work."

"Where is this island?"

"Edges of doldrums, off shipping routes, northeast of here."

"No. Precisely?"

"Why? Too far to swim."

"Too far to swim in one go. Maybe. Too far to swim for you, but if sea elves had a place to rest, even a small boat, just something that floats, that we could hold onto when we got sleepy . . ."

Sea elves, when they got sleepy, cuddled up to a nook in the coral reef somewhere where they could keep their noses out of the water with minimal effort and slept, mostly supported by the water. Hriss looked around. In fact, he was probably in Dunnomian's bed right now. Which reminded him he had his morning necessities to take care of, and this wasn't the place to do it.

"I don't know. We followed Miguel's Path spell to meet the dragon. Then the dragon took us to the island."

Dunnomian wanted to know about the dragon and Hriss begged a few minutes to do the necessary before they got back to talking.

"I wonder where they are," Dunnomian wondered as Hriss was coming back from the necessary.

Location: Port of Bonito, Dragon Lands
Date: 6 Wovoro, 773 AR

Bonito in the morning was a surprisingly clean place. The dragons insisted on it. Something about really big noses and a very sensitive sense of smell.

"We spent two hours at the Nasine royal governor's compound yesterday," Miguel said, stretching as they left the inn, "and established that Lizardfolk island is owned by the lizardfolk and sea elves of Pango Island. The royal governor wasn't thrilled, but with Brazla there to confirm that she'd witnessed the grant in Noron's name, there wasn't a lot he could do unless he wanted to challenge me about it.

"Honestly, I think he was considering it for a minute there. An island that size is a valuable property."

"Oh, he was," Brazla confirmed. "So, shall we go to the port?"

A light two-wheeled cart was waiting by the inn. And a small man in a loincloth and not much else, was standing next to it. "I will take you to the port office." He rubbed his thumb and two fingers together in the age-old gesture for payment. "I will only charge a reasonable fee."

The haggling began in Nasine, and Cordelia let Miguel do it. She spoke Nasine by now, but not all that well. And the man's accent was strange. They ended up taking two of the rickshaws as they were called, Cordelia and Lou in one, and Brazla and Miguel in the other.

* * *

The port was also of stone shaped by dragon magic. It was old, though, and worn. Like any port, this place stunk, and Brazla produced a scented handkerchief to mask the smell a little. There were seven ships in port at the moment, five Nasine, an independent flying a Doichen flag of convenience, and a Kingdom Isles naval ship, though it was not a KOTC ship.

The portmaster stared openly at Lou. He spoke to Miguel without looking away from Lou. "It's one of them sea elves, ain't it, not a mer that's gone halfsies?"

"Yes, I am a sea elf, *human*." Lou was used to that sort of treatment from the humans of Pango Island, but it was clear to Cordelia that he wasn't happy with being an "it" here.

"Pretty full of itself, ain't it?" the portmaster said, still talking to Miguel. "I hear all elves are that way."

"Do you think it would be tasty, Louanomannian?" Brazla asked Lou. "I don't think I've ever had a human quite so greasy as that one."

The portmaster looked at Brazla, then looked again. In his interest in Lou, he'd failed to notice the dragon in human form. Now he did. Brazla looked human enough to pass casual examination, but her skin, on closer examination, had a metallic sheen to it and its color was the yellow of brass. Her hair looked like spun brass, with perhaps a bit more copper in it. But, most of all, her dragon scale dress was a dead giveaway.

155

"Your pardon, ma'am," the portmaster said quickly. "Your folk rarely come to the port, and even more rarely in human form. Is it one of yours?"

Cordelia shook her head. The man wasn't trying to be rude. He, once he'd identified Brazla as a dragon, was clearly trying to be polite. He just couldn't fathom that a sea elf should be treated as a person. Cordelia recognized the pattern from her first encounters with humans interacting with elves. They knew what they knew, and weren't going to be swayed by the evidence of their eyes.

"Let it go," she told both elf and dragon. "Portmaster, what ships are available for lease with crew?"

"Lease, is it, Missy?" Again the man spoke before looking. Cordelia was again dressed in her wizard's robes, with the silver and orange embroidery of her wizard rank. Even in a place like this, wizards weren't common, and a wizard in the company of a dragon wouldn't be wearing robes above her station. That would be *unwise*. "Ma'am, Journeyman wizard, that is."

"Ships?" Cordelia repeated. "Large enough to take a couple of hundred passengers on a trip of several weeks."

"Preferably Nasine flagged," Miguel added.

"I don't think anything in port right now would suit your needs, but the *Ala de Mar* is expected in a few days. She's a large cargo hauler, but could carry passengers in a pinch."

"What's it carrying now?"

"Goods from Nasine. Mixed bag, clocks, magical engines, swords, armor. You know the best swords in the world are made in Nasine," he added with pride. "Also pots, pans, and most anything made of steel."

Nasine did have a flourishing iron and steel industry that was facilitated by their interest in war and the tools of war.

"And what is in the harbor now?" Brazla asked.

He described the ships and he was right. They weren't suitable. Mostly they weren't big enough, or sea worthy enough. They were mostly coastal traders who needed to be able to go into shore to avoid high seas.

Location: Port of Bonito, Dragon Lands
Date: 9 Wovoro, 773AR

The *Ala de Mar* arrived, and on the docks to meet it were Brazla and her party.

The captain, Stefano de Castro, was a Nasine hidalgo who had worked his way up from ensign to captain. He maintained the traditions of martial prowess, but was, in everyday practice, a merchant skipper.

Recognizing Miguel as an intercessor of Noron, he invited them all to his cabin. More worldly-wise than the portmaster, he examined them all. "I am honored to see such a, ah, diverse group aboard my ship." He gave them each a florid bow, including Lou in the little off the cuff ceremony, then made sure each of his guests was seated comfortably and sent his ensign, a nephew of his lady, off for beverages and savories.

"Now, gentles, among such a group, it is beyond my poor powers of observation to say who has precedence. Intercessor, in Noron's name, I beg your indulgence. Who is the leader of your party?"

"I doubt not that your powers of observation would be adequate in any normal circumstances, Captain. Here, well, it's a challenge. The wizard, Cordelia Cooper, is on a quest to right a wrong done to her friends and associates. The sea elf, Louanomannian, is a leader of his people who are victimized by that same injustice. And of course, last but never least, is the Brass Dragon Brazla, who has joined our quest for her own reasons."

"And you? Even given your youth and the august company you travel in, you are an intercessor of Noron. And doesn't that pip on your collar indicate that the god of contests grants you spells? Surely you deserve some mention in the tale?"

Cordelia noted in silence that it was getting pretty deep in here.

"Not much. I am Miguel Cordoba, a student of theology at the University of Kronisberg, and upon hearing the nature of her quest, I at first sought only to dissuade her from it. Then, on praying on the matter, came to realize that she had the right of it. Which conclusion Noron clearly agreed with, for it was those very prayers that brought my first spells."

"I must hear the round tale," Stefano de Castro insisted, and with a grin added, "Perhaps I too will first want to persuade you to abandon the quest, young wizardess." He gave Cordelia a seated bow. And a big grin.

"I expect you will," Cordelia agreed, but her returning smile was a little forced.

He nodded again to Cordelia, then looked to Miguel. "So, tell me, Intercessor Cordoba, what made you disapprove?"

Miguel told the tale, including why he disapproved and why he came to approve, what he had found on the trip and, especially, what he'd found on Pango Island.

Miguel was a good speaker and Cordelia found that some of his insights were interesting even though she'd been there.

"So after justifying her piracy against the—" Stefano held up his hands. "—admitted smuggler, you would have me commit the same crime?"

"Not at all," Cordelia broke in. "KOTC regulations do not restrict the transport of people, just of goods for sale.

"You won't be transporting these people to sell them, will you, Captain?" And this time Cordelia's smile wasn't forced, but it was very hard.

"I would not dare it, young wizard."

"Wise of you," Brazla said with a little laugh.

"But I doubt that the governor of Pango would share your interpretation of KOTC law. Nor am I sure that the commercial courts of the KOTC would find in my favor should another Cordelia capture my ship."

He sighed. "I concede, Intercessor, that Noron probably does approve of your quest. But I have a ship to run and expenses to make good on. I owe the bankers here and in Nasine quite a bit, and the ship needs recaulking, or will soon. I simply can't afford to take my ship out of action for the months it would take to transport so many. And that doesn't include the risk to myself, my ship, and my crew. I would accept the risk to myself as a matter of course, being a gentleman of Nasine, but I can't do the same with the ship or, most especially, the crew."

And the bargaining began. It went on for some time and occasionally got loud, but never really acrimonious. It also grew to include Brazla, for much of the fee would be her money, and Cordelia, because of the Tug spell, which Captain de Castro very much wanted. And Lou, because half the people to be transported would be his people and because he was empowered to make bargains in regard to trade with the captain.

The Dragon Lands grew several teas that were popular in Centraium, as well as other products. So there was regular trade back and forth and profit to be made. To take de Castro's ship out of the trade for what amounted to months of back and forth between Lizardfolk Island and Pango Island would cost them. Captain de Castro wanted exclusive trading rights. Brazla pointed out that refusing to trade with ships that came to Lizardfolk Island was risky at best. And on and on, back and forth, until they reached an agreement.

The lizardfolk would build a dock and the *Ala de Mar* would have no docking fees for two, no, four years, because it was going to take the lizardfolk and the sea elves time to set up any farming industries.

But trade wouldn't be restricted to the *Ala de Mar* or even only to Nasine ships. An amount of Brazla's gold would go to the *Ala de Mar*. How much depended on how many trips the *Ala de Mar* ended up making.

Cordelia would do the inlays to make the prow of the *Ala de Mar* into a magical item that could be charged with the Tug spell. And Noron would give Miguel the spell to age the prow so that the spell would always be ready.

"I can ask, but I cannot compel Noron," Miguel said at that.

"Well then, let's see how much Noron approves of this venture. We'll make it contingent on Noron's approval in the form of the ageing spell," Stefano de Castro said piously. "After all, I could never take on such a quest if, in fact, Noron doesn't approve."

"Noron isn't a god who makes bargains," Miguel warned, sounding as self-righteous as he had back in Kronisburg.

"No, but the judge of contests respects both courage and skill. Or so I was taught as a child. So I'm minded to take my chances."

"Also, Miguel is a very young intercessor," Cordelia pointed out. "He gets spells, but not spells that powerful. The spell he cast before didn't age the prow item all at once. Instead, it caused it to age faster. I think it's unlikely that Noron is going to burn out one of his intercessors because you want a permanent Tug spell."

Miguel visibly bristled at the young comment, but kept silent.

Captain de Castro looked at Cordelia and Miguel, then slowly nodded. "All I ask is the same spell cast before, and I'll buy the pig. Just an assurance that this *is* Noron's will."

And it was settled. De Castro ended up paying for the magic moss and his ship's carpenter did the carving. It took about a week to get everything ready. Miguel did get a spell that was similar, but not identical, to the one he cast before and he cast it on the prow of the *Ala de Mar*.

Location: *Ala de Mar, Dragon Lands*
Date: *17 Wovoro, 773 AR*

The *Ala de Mar* pulled out of harbor not by the Tug spell built into the prow, but by Cordelia's Tug spell cast on the hull of the ship, far enough from the other to not interfere with its magic. It took them two weeks beating mostly up wind to get to the vicinity of Pango Island.

And they had another problem. They didn't want the *Ala de Mar* sitting in sight of Pango Island while they negotiated with the lizardfolk. The solution was simple enough. The *Ala de Mar* would dock at an island that was owned by a dragon of Brazla's acquaintance, and they would take a ship's boat to Pango Island.

The dragon in question had, out of politeness, agreed not to eat the crew of the *Ala de Mar*, as long as they stayed on the ship or the ship's boat.

Location: *Off Pango Island*
Date: *1 Estormany, 773 AR*

The ship's boat, being pulled by the Tug spell, approached the coral reef near the Tomson Plantation, and Lou went over the side. Only to return a few minutes later with another sea elf.

Dunnomian grabbed the gunnell of the small boat and said, "We thought that you had betrayed us. Well, I thought you'd betrayed us. Hriss was afraid you were lost at sea.

"We have rafts ready to make the trip to the island if you have directions?"

What followed was a five minute discussion of sea conditions . . . or who knows what . . . in Sea Elvish, which is a unique language with various words for the density and salinity of seawater, the shape of the currents flowing through it, and things a human would be completely unaware of.

Finally, Dunnomian nodded. "That should be enough, but you are going to have a time convincing the lizardfolk to go. They don't have a lot of faith in you," he said to Cordelia, "since everyone who deals with you ends up worse off."

As guilty as Cordelia felt about what had happened, she was getting tired of getting the blame from the lizardfolk. And the sea elves and, well, everyone. "Well then, that will be up to them. We've arranged transport, but if they don't want to go, I'm not going to be forcing anyone." She looked at Dunnomian. "And that goes for you sea elves as well. I have done my best for you. Taken the better part of a year away from my studies, and at this point any . . . Never mind. Go or stay as it suits you, on your own responsibility."

Dunnomian gave her a hard look, but after a long moment, he nodded. "Very well. Follow me."

He led them to another section of reef, where a cold, and therefore sleepy, lizardman was sleeping on the reef, because no place on the island was truly safe for him.

* * *

"Our escape put the wyvern among the pogan. And, by now, the news of Lizardfolk Island has reached the authorities," Hriss said.

"How are they reacting to that?"

"They panicss!" Hriss said, caught between glee and terror. "Governor made proclamation. Flat illegal, not just Kingdom law, but KOTC regulations. And going to get out. May take while, but will get out. Too many humans know to hush up."

"What sort of proclamation?"

"He declared it illegal for a lizardman leave plantation where he works without permission of plantation owner."

Cordelia shook her head in confusion. "How is that different at all?"

"Because only thing kept contract employment plantations from being slavery was right leave. We had right leave, but no place. We had right go, no place go. Right, but no way use. Without right leave is slavery. And all illegal."

Which reminded Cordelia again that, whatever his speech patterns, Hriss had a deep and clear understanding of the laws and regulations of the Kingdom Isles and the KOTC.

"Which could bring the Kingdom down on the KOTC. And that is something the KOTC can't abide. I understand. If we bring a ship in the way that the Nasine smuggler came in, will the lizardfolk of the Tomson Plantation come away with us? Or will they follow the governor's proclamation?"

"Don't know." Hriss shook his head. "Some want go. Some want stay. I think most want go, but afraid."

Hriss climbed aboard the dinghy, Cordelia cast Tug again, and they headed back to the dragon's island and the ship.

CHAPTER 14

Location: Ala de Mar, Dragon Kirbath's Island
Date: 2 Estormany, 773AR

The *Ala de Mar* sailed away from Kirbath's Island the next afternoon, tacking against an unfriendly wind. Even with the Tug spell cast by Cordelia, it was going to take a long time to cover the eighty plus miles from Kirbath's Island to Pango Island. Because tacking upwind, they would travel a longer distance.

The good news was that the weather was closing in and it looked to be a foggy night. That gave the captain pause, but Lou assured him that he would know the seas as they approached Pango. He would feel it in the breeze and smell it in the air.

Still nervous, but not really doubting, the captain agreed. The knowledge of sea elves wasn't questioned in this part of the world.

* * *

As they arrived in the predawn off Pango, Lou dove over the side, cutting the water with little in the way of a splash. An hour later, he was back. A rope ladder was tossed down, and Lou climbed up. He then guided the ship the rest of the way into the docks at the Tomson-now-Williams plantation.

Location: Williams Plantation
Date: 3 Estormany, 773AR

As the crew of the ship was throwing ropes to the pier, Hriss was chivvying his people out to the ship. Not all of them. There had been discussion, and of the slightly over two hundred lizardfolk who worked on the plantation, just over a hundred wanted to go. The problem was that those who stayed would likely be punished by Williams for the leaving of the hundred, so there were another fifty or so who chose to go because they didn't want to be here when it was discovered that the others had left. That left fifty-three who flat out refused to go. And, for now, they were tied up in the quarters, a set of connected shacks, out of sight of the main house.

The lizardfolk knew each other. For the most part, they had grown up and lived their entire lives on this plantation. Some of them had lived here for upwards of two hundred years. They knew who was honest and who wasn't, who would want to sell out the others to protect themselves. And all of those eight were tied up in the shacks or under close watch.

But nothing is perfect. They were all busy loading up stuff. Even what amounts to a slave can accumulate a few things over decades and centuries. They were all carrying packs, some of seeds and cuttings to start plants on the new island, others with keepsakes and doodads that had been gathered over their lives. Moving silently isn't easy for that many people, even in the best of circumstances, and these weren't the best of circumstances.

Mrs. Amelia Williams woke as her husband was getting out of bed. She hadn't been sleeping well since that girl had come back to the island. It was all Cordelia Cooper's fault, really. It was Cordelia who killed William. It was Cordelia who convinced her to take on the responsibility of seeing to the legalities and managing the prize money. And they were all perfectly legitimate expenses. The plantation had expenses, and boarding school in the Kingdom Isles was exceedingly expensive, and Robert had his own debts that simply had to be dealt with. It wasn't Amelia's fault that the legitimate expenses had consumed the entire prize and more. Even if some of the bookkeeping was a little uncertain.

It all would have worked out if Cordelia Cooper had just stayed away.

And it wasn't like she was going to need the money. She was already a wizard and wizards were all rich.

But no. She had to get on her high horse and insist that the sea elves and lizardfolk get their share, like lizardfolk had any need for money. They were well taken care of and their reptile brains weren't up to the management—

There was a noise from outside. "What was that, Robert?"

"How am I supposed to know? There have been noises for the last fifteen minutes or so, but you were too drunk to notice, as usual."

"I'm doing my best."

Robert, already mostly dressed, pulled on his left boot and stood. "Get up and go wake the servants, you lazy slut. I'm going to want breakfast after I see to whatever's going on out there."

* * *

Robert Williams had lately been wondering just how good a plan marrying Amelia was. It had retired his debts well enough and gotten him in good with the governor, but the way those debts were retired couldn't bear scrutiny. Any sort of an investigation performed by anyone other than the governor's accountants would land him in prison because the money he'd paid to himself was absurd.

Especially the money beyond that which the prize brought. That was the governor's idea. A tool to keep Cooper from coming back to the island.

He opened the front door to see a three-masted schooner tied up to the dock. He turned back into the house and grabbed his sword. Robert wasn't craven. He understood the world. You took what you could get and you protected what was yours. That was the way the world worked, unless you wanted to end your life as a beggar sleeping in an alley.

And he had one hard and fast rule.

Robert took from others. *No one* took from Robert.

He ran out onto the veranda and saw a line of lizardfolk boarding the ship. *NO! This is not happening. Not to me.* He leapt down the steps and, bellowing orders, ran for the docks.

To manage an estate this big required overseers and trustees. There were three overseers, humans, and fifteen trustees, lizardfolk. The humans lived in the main house and the lizardfolk lived in the shacks. The lizardfolk trustees weren't going to be coming to Robert's aid. They were tied up in the shacks, with gags to keep them quiet.

The three overseers came boiling out of the house in various stages of undress, carrying whips and short knives. They were there to discipline lizardfolk, not to fight a ship full of armed men, a bunch of sea elves, and the young woman that one of them recognized as Cordelia Cooper. They came boiling out of the house all right, but they stopped on the veranda.

Robert didn't stop. He was much too angry to pay attention to such things.

✻ ✻ ✻

Brazla, in lizardwoman form again, was watching the lizardfolk board the ship. At the noise, she moved up the pier to see what the human wanted.

He swung at her.

He swung at me! He tried to kill me!

Brazla was a moderately powerful dragon with a fair amount of magic, and in her natural form, a sword like the one the fool had swung at her wouldn't even sting unless he got lucky, and hit someplace delicate.

But she wasn't in her normal form. She was in the form of an attractive young lizard woman. And in that form, a sword like that could have seriously injured her. It could have *killed* her. For just a fleeting instant Brazla was more frightened than she'd been in three hundred years.

Then she was *furious*.

In the blink of an eye, the five foot two lizard woman turned into a dragon whose head was bigger than that. "How dare you, you worm!" she bellowed, and along with her words came a billow of flame that engulfed Robert Willams and scorched several other people, two sea elves, four lizardfolk, and a human crewman off the *Ala de Mar*.

Robert Williams was burning. Well, his clothing was burning. His skin was blistering. And he was running.

Running from a dragon is never a good idea. They are instinctive hunters.

Running from an angry dragon is an even worse idea.

Brazla was still furious. She didn't hesitate. She simply reached out her neck, and snapped. That took care of the running, as his legs were gone. One quick swallow, and another snap. Another swallow, and Robert

Williams was gone, except for a bit of fluid on Brazla's snout. And a delicate lick with her eight-foot-long forked tongue took care of that.

✳ ✳ ✳

Cordelia looked around, then called, "Miguel, do what you can for the wounded."

"Right, Cordelia," Miguel said, coming out of his moment of shock. It had all happened so fast.

Miguel was fast and well trained, but this was different. There is a difference between a set duel and combat that comes out of nowhere. And while he had trained for the second, he'd never experienced it.

There was plenty of time for Cordelia to react. Miguel got to work on the wounded.

The dragon was still sitting on the shore with her tail in the water. And no one else was moving. Finally, as Miguel was applying bandages, the lizardfolk began to move again, some of them bowing with great respect to the dragon, and the rest getting onto the ship just as fast as they could.

There wasn't panic. Lizardfolk consider dragons to be the next things to gods and even if Brazla wasn't their god, she was still a dragon. Being told that a dragon witnessed and confirmed the grant of Lizardfolk Island and seeing the dragon are two different things.

Once the scorched were bandaged and what little healing Miguel could do was done, he came over to Cordelia. "Something about all this bothers me."

"Something about a dragon eating a human in front of you bothers you? How surprising!"

"Not that!" Miguel brushed the air like he was brushing away a fly. "It's the rest of it. And it's been bothering me since we got to Pango and everyone went crazy."

"What do you mean?"

"They care too much."

"What are you talking about?"

"There's this argument that I've been having with the intercessors of Cashi and Justain since I got to Kronisburg. About the difference between contracts, law, and right. Cashi's followers are all about the wording of a contract. And if they can put one over on you in a deal, they aren't ashamed of it. They are proud of it. They say things like 'He'd buy a three-legged horse' as though that justified stealing from someone."

"I tend to agree about Cashi, but what does that have to do with anything?"

"Why did they lock you up instead of laughing at you?" Miguel asked. "Why weren't you snubbed and presented with a bill for services rendered? Why arrested and told you would stay locked up until you signed your agreement to the governor's findings? Why search the island for an intercessor of Noron and a fool who bought a three-legged horse?"

"So why?"

"Because this wasn't a valid contract. Or because they broke the contract in some way. Cordelia, I think you really ought to insist on access to the books of your agent here on the island." He looked at the main house significantly.

Brazla's head turned, following Miguel's gaze, and the three overseers who were still standing on the veranda started backing away. Brazla opened her mouth. Whips and knives were dropped, and the overseers backed faster. Then one turned and ran. The other two followed.

Brazla snorted a fifteen foot flame and took human form in the blink of an eye, then came over to join Cordelia and Miguel. Lou also came down the gangplank to join them. He had some things to say to Amelia Williams as well. Things about his sister and his people.

* * *

Amelia Williams was watching from a window, terrified. They were going to kill her. She knew it. But it wasn't her fault. None of it was her fault. She was convinced of that. She'd had years to convince herself of that and she was very good at convincing herself that things weren't her fault.

They didn't knock, just opened the door and came in like they owned the place. The main house was a large single-story house on four-foot pilings, stairs up to the veranda and the whole house off the ground to get the full advantages of the sea breezes. When they entered the room where she was, what popped out of her mouth was, "I didn't order Irela's whipping! I would never do that!"

"No, but you stood by while Williams ordered it," Lou said in disgust. "You do a lot of standing by while others do your dirty work."

"It's not my fault," Amelia insisted. "None of it is my fault. You don't know the pressures I was under. I had to protect my son. I had to see to his welfare."

"I don't care anymore why you did the things you did," Cordelia said. "Where are the accounts? I want to see the books, all the transactions you or any of your agents made in the matters regarding the valuation of the Nasine ship taken while smuggling."

Amelia's eyes went to a large rosewood file cabinet against one wall of the room, and then she said, "Those are in the city. At Government House."

Lou asked, "Is she telling the truth, Miguel?"

Miguel looked at Lou in confusion for just a moment, then said sadly, "No, I am afraid not." Noron was fine with feints and misdirection in a sword fight, a battle, or a debate. He was the god of contests, not the god of truth.

"Miguel is an intercessor of Noron, and he gets spells. You won't be able to get a lie past him. Now where are the files?"

"They are in town," she said, "but there are copies in the cabinet."

Cordelia walked over to the cabinet and Amelia said, "Those are private property."

Cordelia said, "My property."

"She believes it," Miguel said, referring to Amelia. "I think, just as a matter of form, we want her to officially grant permission to examine the files and even take them with us."

"I won't!"

"I'm still feeling a bit peckish," Brazla said. "That fool with the sword wasn't all that satisfying."

Amelia looked at the woman . . . no, the dragon in human form. "You can have anything you want."

"Why, thank you," Cordelia said.

"She tends to forget promises that she's made," Lou pointed out. "Promises to you, promises to the lizardfolk, promises to us. All forgotten as soon as a flatterer smiles her way."

"In that case, we probably need the permission in writing. Just as a reminder of what was said. I can manage that." Miguel went over to the desk, sat down, found paper, took a pen and dipped it in the inkwell and began to write in a smooth and flowing script.

It took a few minutes and several dips in the inkwell.

"What are you writing?" Lou asked, "a book?"

"I just don't want to leave anything out."

173

"We're going to need some crew to carry this load. It's rather too much for a human to read in a few minutes."

And it was. The records of Amelia's actions as Cordelia's agent took two and a half drawers in the fancy file cabinet.

"I'll go see about that," Lou said.

"Wait a moment," Miguel said. "I want you to act as witness while Mrs. Williams signs the permission. The rest of us too." He stood as he was speaking, turned and handed Amelia the pen.

Giving Brazla a quick look, Amelia sat and signed. Then she looked at the sheet, and in spite of her fear, snorted a bitter laugh. "Without coercion?"

"Has anyone here threatened you?" Miguel asked.

It was true. No one had said a word that was a threat. Even the dragon had just said that she was feeling peckish, not that she was going to burn Amelia alive and gobble her down in two bites.

❊ ❊ ❊

It took a few minutes for them to get some of the crew of the *Ala de Mar* to carry out the files. And after Brazla had a talk with the lizardfolk who were tied up, about half of them decided to go. Leaving a spice plantation that took two hundred lizardfolk to operate with just twenty-seven.

Brazla wasn't threatening, not to the lizardfolk. It was more her assurance that there really was an island, that it was really theirs, and that *a* dragon—if not necessarily *their* dragon—approved of the move that convinced them.

CHAPTER 15

Location: Ala de Mar, off Lizardfolk Island
Date: 10 Estormany, 773 AR

It had been a miserable trip. The *Ala de Mar* was not a passenger ship. It wasn't even a big cargo ship. A hundred seventy-seven lizardfolk and thirty-seven sea elves were more than it was set up for. Add in mostly all the worldly goods of the refugees, as little as those were, and the *Ala de Mar* was packed to the scuppers.

Stefano de Castro looked at the ring of coral reefs around the island. He'd circled the entire island and not seen a gap. "I can't take the Ala de Mar in there."

"No, not yet, Captain. And you won't be able to even after we have opened ways through the reef, not without our granting passage. For now, just anchor here and use the small boats to take the lizardfolk to the island," Lou said.

"That's going to make it a week to unload," the captain said, exaggerating.

Lizardfolk Island was an oval, about ten miles north to south and six east to west, a bit thicker at the south end, like a lopsided egg. It was surrounded, at a distance of from a mile to half a mile, by a ring of coral reefs that had built up over the centuries. The reef was between a hundred and five hundred feet wide, and actually broke the surface at low tide over half the time. In fact, there were gaps in the reef, but none were wide enough and straight enough for a ship with the length and draft of the *Ala de Mar* to pass through. The reef, even as it stood now, represented a fortress wall around the island, protecting it from seaborne attack. That was part of the reason that Miguel had assumed it would be a good home for the lizardfolk and sea elves.

Coral is a complex ecology all on its own. Living stone. It is made up of deposits of shells of living creatures and builds up over time from small outcroppings to huge barriers. In this world, with its magic that was based on the complexity of life, coral was more than that. It was as inherently magical as amber, jet, or bone. In some ways, more so. It was as alive as the core of a tree, which was why it could be used as a resting and restoring place for sea elves. And, like a tree, its growth could be modified by the elves that inhabited it.

Over time—quite a lot of time by human standards, but quite quickly by the way elves measure time—this complex of reefs would become an elven city as full of life and diversity as any forest or jungle above the surface. Lou could see it, even if Captain de Castro couldn't.

Over the next day and a half, the two jolly boats that the *Ala de Mar* carried and the skiff that they had left on the island were used to ferry lizardfolk to the island, and sea elves found their places in the reef, the hollows and nooks where they would rest when not swimming or hunting in the lagoon between the reef and the island. It was a rich and vibrant hunting ground, with its own share of predators. The sea elves would make their peace with the dolphins and killer whales, but the sharks were going to have to be thinned drastically.

On the island, the lizardfolk were finding good and bad. It was a lot of land, twenty-five square miles. More than enough for all the lizardfolk that were involved with Cordelia in the taking of the smuggler, but not nearly enough for all the lizardfolk on Pango Island.

On the other hand, there was nothing built here. No plantations with neat and orderly fields, no houses, no egg houses to keep the lizardfolk eggs warm while they waited to hatch. No stoves or toilets, nothing.

"If you want it," Hriss was saying to his fiancee, Ssiris, "we'll build it. But not today. For now, we are going to have to use the forest end, off the beach.

"It's scary back there. Who knows what lives back in that jungle?"

She had a point, Hriss knew, because they hadn't explored the island before Miguel declared it theirs. "I could ask Brazla?"

"No. *I* will ask Brazla!" Ssiris said, and marched off to do that.

Brazla was in lizardwoman form on the island. Hriss didn't know how many forms she had, but she certainly had human and lizardfolk that she could change to at will. And in each of them, she was a quite attractive female. It was something that a lizardman couldn't help but notice, and a lizardwoman even more so. Ssiris had noticed Brazla's appearance on the trip, and not with approval.

✳ ✳ ✳

Ssiris wasn't a fan of the dragon, even if she was a dragon. She especially wasn't fond of a pretty female spending time talking to Hriss. She wasn't as adventurous as Hriss, but she loved him in spite of the fact that he was crazy. She hadn't wanted him to go off to Pango town to be a guide. She hadn't wanted him to get involved in taking the smuggler, either. You had to be pragmatic to avoid that sort of thing, and Hriss wasn't pragmatic. All that, she could put up with, and would.

But a female dragon going after her man? Not happening.

And she'd made that plain on the ship. So Hriss was manipulating her when he offered to ask Brazla about what lived on Lizardfolk Island. She knew it, but it still worked.

By the time she'd gone through that, she'd reached the dragon, who was lying on the sand, still in lizardwoman form, in a pose that could only be called languid. She marched right up to Brazla and asked, "What lives on the island?"

Brazla blinked, shook sensuously, and sat up. "What?"

"What lives on the island? Are there wild dogs? Hogs? Snakes? What?"

"I haven't the faintest idea."

"What? You gave us this island and you don't know what's on it?"

"I didn't give you this island." She pointed at Miguel, who was a couple of hundred feet down the beach, teaching a small group of lizardfolk to use a sword. "He did. All I did was witness the grant."

"But you brought him here."

"As a comfortable place to chat about magic. Not as a permanent home. I can tell you that there is nothing on the island large enough or dangerous enough to bother a dragon while she's chatting. But more than that, you're going to have to discover for yourselves."

The dragon gave Ssiris a look that made her feel small and foolish, like a baby just out of the egg. "Freedom doesn't mean you have everything handed to you on a silver platter. Even freedom on your own island doesn't mean that. Freedom means you build it yourself with no one to tell you you can't. If you don't build it yourself or make something you can sell to buy it, you do without it. You want to know what's on the island? Fine. Go explore the island! No, I guess not. You're lizardfolk. Get together with other lizardfolk and go explore the island as a group."

Not at all happy with the situation, Ssiris proceeded to do just that.

* * *

Over the next two months, the *Ala de Mar* made six more trips between Pango Island and Lizardfolk Island. By the time it was done, there were over a thousand lizardfolk from fifteen Pango Island plantations on Lizardfolk Island, and a small lizardfolk town was located on the north end of the island, at a place they called Gray Rock because of the large granite shelf that stuck out of the ground. It was three hundred feet long and eight wide and warmed to almost scorching in the afternoon on sunny days.

CHAPTER 16

Location: Pango Island
Date: 8 Estormany, 773AR

Т**he chief constable came into the governor's office, too agitated to be properly deferential. "It's confirmed, Governor. Most of the lizards on the Williams plantation are gone and, if the stories are to be believed, a dragon ate Robert Williams. And along with the dragon were that Cooper woman and the Nasine intercessor."

"What about the sea elves?" Governor Hopkins asked. Rumors had been circulating for two days.

"They were involved, Governor. A bunch of them from the reefs near the Williams plantation are gone. And you know that they kidnapped that sea elf tutor that Tomson kept for his son."

"Where did they go?"

"Apparently to an island some days travel by sea." The constable, without permission, went over and sat on the couch next to the door. He rubbed his face. "So far, the rumors about that are pretty vague. It's north of here, probably to the northeast, but no one knows how far east, and there is a lot of ocean between here and Amonrai."

"That skiff didn't go all the way to Amonrai, not in the time they had."

"That's the other problem. We don't actually know how many trips they made. We don't know if the lizard was actually with them when they left the island after they escaped. The stories say he was, but we didn't catch him, so we couldn't ask him. From the timing of the stealing of your skiff to the kidnapping of the sea elf, it would seem it was about ten days round trip. Five days there and five back, or less in a skiff. It's got to be fairly close."

"The winds have been westerlies for the last month, you moron. If the island was that close, you could climb a tree and see it." Andrew was exaggerating, but not all that much.

With a skiff in these conditions, given the single sail of the skiff, they could sail rapidly from west to due north, but anything much east of due north and they would be spending all their time beating upwind. So an island to the northeast would have to be very close. If it was seven days against the wind to get there and three with the wind to get back, you're still talking no more than five hundred miles. Assuming they went, turned right around, and came back. And there weren't any islands worth the name in that chunk of ocean.

And yet the sea elf went missing ten days after the skiff went— Andrew Hopkins knew what had happened. "The northeast, my butt. They went to Kirbath's Island. The damned dragons are making a play for the islands."

"They'd never do it."

The weakness of the Dragon Lands was the constant squabbling of the dragons. There was no cohesion, no group action. Any dragon could do anything, and no dragon was in any great hurry to do much of anything. Before the Nasine and Kingdom folk showed up, the dragons were even worse. The common threat had forced the dragons to semi-common cause. Enough to make a deal with the KOTC and another with the Nasine Empire. Sort of a "leave us alone and we'll leave you alone" deal. And the dragons enforced the deal on other dragons, mostly because they didn't want to be bothered by a major war. So what happened here had to be that Kirbath was trying to take Pango Island away from the KOTC.

"That's why the Cooper girl came back. She has some sort of deal with Kirbath.

"What ships do we have in port?" The governor knew the answer before he got the question out. It was rare that they had more than three ships in harbor at any given time. At the moment, there was just one. "Have Johnson take the *Dragon Clipper* to Bellamy and lodge a formal complaint against Kirbath for murder and invasion."

"Governor, you can't. The penalty for a false accusation . . ."

"It's not false."

The penalty for a false accusation against a dragon was essentially that the dragon got carte blanche to do what it was accused of. Accuse a dragon of stealing a treasure and be wrong, the dragon now had permission to steal a treasure of equal value. Accuse a dragon of murder and invasion, the dragon had the right to murder and invade. If the accusation was proved true, the dragons would punish the offending dragon, usually with death. But if it wasn't, the accuser was screwed. And if he made the accusation against Kirbath and Kirbath wasn't guilty . . . well, Kirbath would be able to kill his accuser and invade Pango Island without repercussions. And even if he decided not to, he would be in a position to demand what amounted to a massive tribute from the KOTC. A lot of tribute.

"Governor, you have to be sure. You have to find a witness. Something."

"All right. Send a squad and bring back Amelia Williams. And at least a couple of lizards that saw the incident."

Location: Pango Island
Date: 13 Estormany, 773AR

Amelia Williams, in the ten days since the encounter with the peckish dragon, had determined whose fault it all was. She couldn't blame Cordelia Cooper. Not because of the justice of the situation, but because Amelia was utterly incapable of blaming anything on someone who kept company with a peckish dragon. That sort of thinking led to ending up as dragon snack food.

It was the governor's fault.

He was the one who hadn't just paid off Cordelia. He was the one who had introduced her to Robert. He was the one who had orchestrated the whole mess, including the idea that Cordelia owed her money as a way of keeping the girl from coming back and insisting on looking at the books.

So when she was escorted—none too gently—into the governor's office, she wasn't in a mood to be cooperative. "What is the meaning of this? A dragon kills my husband and you send your goons to drag me here? It won't do you any good to have me sign anything. Cordelia has my copies of the books and a letter giving her permission to take them."

"Why on earth would you write a letter like that?"

"I didn't write it. That Nasine intercessor wrote it, and had me sign it. As to why I signed it, well, Governor, you aren't nearly as scary as a dragon who just ate my husband and is feeling 'a bit peckish.' "

"I knew it. It was Kirbath."

As it happened, Amelia knew perfectly well that it wasn't Kirbath. Kirbath was male and a red dragon, not a female brass dragon. And Kirbath was considerably smaller, only around a hundred feet long, not the hundred and fifty of Brazla. But Amelia wasn't in any mood to cooperate with the greedy fool who had caused all this. On the other hand, she didn't want to tell a lie that would come back on her. She kept quiet.

"It was Kirbath, wasn't it?"

"I really can't say. It all happened so fast. And when the dragon was in my living room, it was in human form."

The interview wasn't conclusive by any means, but Andrew Hopkins had apparently made up his mind about what had happened before she ever got there. He sent her away.

* * *

After hearing Amelia's story, and especially the part about permission to take the books for examination, Andrew Hopkins knew he had to make the complaint. It was his only chance. If the stuff in those records got back to the Kingdom Isles, he was going to jail.

He sent the ship.

CHAPTER 17

Location: Lizardfolk Island
Date: 17 Cashi, 773 AR

C ordelia looked at the village. It was a nice place in its way. Several wood buildings with leaf roofs, quite well made. Yes, it was a nice place, and would get even nicer over time. Several more trips to Pango Island had brought more lizardfolk and more sea elves. It was a viable population, and between Hriss, Lou, the council made up of sea elves and lizardfolk, and Miguel, who had decided to stay to teach these people how to defend their island, it looked to be a good situation.

She looked over at the large brass dragon lying on the beach, checked her pack one last time, and said, "Okay, Brazla. I'm ready."

Brazla turned into a human woman in the blink of an eye and put a hand on Cordelia's shoulder.

Location: Kronisberg, Centraium
Date: 17 Cashi, 773 AR
It was midafternoon rather than early evening, but it was also the middle of Cashi in the northern hemisphere. It was not much above freezing in

the street outside Das Vizart's Dank. And neither Cordelia nor Brazla was dressed for it. They went in quickly.

Meggie looked up as the bell over the door announced them. "Cordelia! When did you get back?"

"Just this minute," Cordelia said, rubbing her hands over her sleeves to try and warm up. It was warm in the taproom compared to outside, but not compared to the eighty plus degrees of Lizardfolk Island. She and Brazla moved toward the fire at the far end of the tap room.

"This is Brazla. She's here to learn book wizardry." Cordelia stopped for a moment, and looked around the room. It was between the lunch and dinner rushes. Not many people in the tap room at this time of day. It was just the three of them. "She's a brass dragon," Cordelia finished, watching Meggie while she stood next to the large fireplace trying to get warm.

Meggie's eyes got big, but she took a breath and said, "What can I get you?"

Brazla, not looking at Meggie, said, "Do you serve knight in shining armor?"

Meggie's eyes got bigger and Cordelia could tell that she wasn't sure that Brazla was joking. Cordelia wasn't totally sure herself, but she said, "Whatever you have in the pot, Meggie. When a dragon is in human form they eat the same amount that a human eats. Well, mostly. Brazla eats like a horse, but stays thin."

They spent the afternoon getting acquainted and, for a while, Brazla would be staying at the inn.

Location: School of Law, University of Kronisberg, Centraium
Date: 18 Cashi, 773 AR

The same young law student was on duty in the entry hall.

Master Harris still looked much too young and innocent to be a third year student, much less a fourth year, as he must be by now.

"What have you brought me this time, Journeywoman Cooper?"

"More of the same, I'm afraid. I have the account books from the prize court. And from their actions, I think there must be something in them."

"I do hope you didn't steal them. There are rules about that sort of thing. We won't be able to use them if they were obtained illegally. And you could be extradited to the Kingdom Isles over theft, as you wouldn't be over failure to pay debts."

"No. Right at the top, I have permission to take them, signed by Amelia Williams, who was supposed to be my agent there."

She passed over the papers, and Master Harris agreed to look them over. That took a bit of effort. They were in her bag of holding with a lightness spell on them. But as they came out of the bag of holding they resumed their size and weight.

Three days later, she got a note to go back and see him.

The law department agreed to take the case on a contingency basis. There were serious irregularities in the books, but the outcome was uncertain. And, "You probably won't see much after legal fees, even if we win."

"Then why are you willing to take the case?" Cordelia asked.

He grinned like a cherub. "This is a name maker. If we win it, I'll have a reputation as a solicitor who's willing and able to go up against the KOTC."

"Glad I could help," Cordelia said.

Location: School of Theology , University of Kronisberg,
Centraium
Date: 19 Cashi, 773 AR

High Intercessor Sawnell again escorted Cordelia to her meeting with
High Intercessor Alvarez, who was dedicated to Noron.

"Where is Miguel?" High Intercessor Alvarez demanded as soon as they
were through the door.

"On Lizardfolk Island, happily teaching the lizardfolk and sea elves how
to defend their island, in case anyone in the KOTC should contest their
ownership. I have a letter from him here." She passed over the letter, which
Alvarez took with little grace or courtesy.

He read the letter, basically ignoring Cordelia and High Intercessor
Sawnell. Cordelia looked at High Intercessor Sawnell, then at the door, but
High Intercessor Sawnell shook his head slightly and waved at a couple of
chairs.

When he finished with Miguel's letter, which was three pages long, High
Intercessor Alvarez spent three hours questioning Cordelia about
Lizardfolk Island, the sea elves, Miguel's state of health and mind. Then he
finally dismissed her with scant grace.

Location: School of Wizardry, University of Kronisberg,
Centraium
Date: 22 Cashi, 773 AR

Cordelia sat in the lecture hall and prepared to take notes on the
preparation of Hop, a short range translocation spell that would move a
wizard a few hundred feet in an instant. It was similar to the real
translocation spell, but weaker and a fair bit simpler. Things were finally
back to normal.

Brazla appeared in the lecture hall with a pop, and every eye focused on
the woman in a dress of miniature brass dragon scales.

Yep. Everything was back to normal.

EPILOG

Location: Pango Island
Date: 22 Coganie, 773 AR

The governor of Bellamy came down the gangplank onto the docks, looked around and sniffed, then proceeded up the street and onward to the governor's residence. His guards were resplendent in dress uniforms with swords and crossbows, and everyone got out of their way.

"Where is Governor Hopkins?"

"Gone, sir," said Lloyd Bansater, the acting governor of Pango Island. "We got it a week ago from one of the lizards that it was a brass dragon that ate poor Mister Williams. As soon as that was confirmed, a skiff went missing and the governor with it."

The governor of Bellamy, who in normal circumstances would be outranked by the governor of Pango Island, nodded. "Thank Cashi for that anyway. Contract with the dragons or not, I wasn't looking forward to tying a human to Dragon Rock. I can report that he left the island before he got—" He stopped suddenly, and looked at the acting governor. "You're sure? If you're lying, you'll end up on the rock next to him. It's a contract before Cashi, signed in the presence of a dozen senior dragons. I'll have no choice. None at all."

"I'm not lying. I'll swear it under the *See Truth* spell if you want. And while it's possible that he circled around to some other part of the island, it's unlikely. The lizards would be quick to turn him in and he knew it."

"Good. It's not our fault if he got away. We made every effort. We are within the contract. With any luck at all, Kirbath will catch the fool."

"Sir!"

"I said I didn't relish tying him to Dragon Rock, not that he didn't deserve it. Do you know how much it's going to cost us to keep Kirbath from exercising his right to invade Pango? No, of course you don't. It's enough to buy a dozen Kingdom Isles nobles out of debt. And you know how profligate that lot is."

All in all, it was the most uncomfortable and degrading promotion that Lloyd Bansater had received in a long career with the KOTC.

But at the end of it, he was the new governor of Pango Island with orders to, one, rescind the order about lizardfolk leaving the island, and two, to keep his hands off Lizardfolk Island and the reef.

CHARACTERS:

Alberto: Alfonso's father, Carlos' son, innkeeper in Elfsain

Alfonso: Half-elf son of Alberto, innkeeper in Elfsain

Alvarez, Ramon: High Intercessor of Noron

Adrogo, Charles: Plantation owner's son in Arginia

Bansater, Lloyd: acting governor Pango Island

Batuca: Captain of the *Maranho*

Batuca, Elena: Second officer and purser of *Maranho*

Brazla: a brass dragon

Cartwright, Rojer: Deceased wizard, Cordelia's former master

Cooper, Cordelia: Wizard, Natural and Book

Cordoba, Miguel: intercessor of Noron

de Castro, Stefano: Captain of the *Ala de Mer*

Cruz, Ramon: Ensign on the *Maranho,* learns to fly

Dolin: Professor of history

Dugan, Jimmy: tries to arrest Cordelia in Arginia

Dunnomian: sea elf

Galengasi: forest elf, mother of Alfonso in Elfsain

Harris: Master, lawyer at University of Kronisberg

Herlict, Agnesse: A wizard instructor at the university

Hopkins, Andrew: Governor of Pango Island

Hriss: Leader of the Lizardfolk on Lizardfolk Island

Irela: Sea elf, sister of Lou

Louanomannian: Lou for short, leader of the sea elves of Pango Island

Meggie: Daughter of owner of Das Vizart's Dank

Rochester: Captain of the *Costoga*

Sawnell: High Intercessor of Zagrod

Ssiris: Lizardwoman, fiancee of Hriss, lizardman

Williams, Robert: Plantation owner, Pango Island

Williams, Amelia Tomson: wife of Robert Williams

Made in the USA
Las Vegas, NV
15 November 2021

34451696R10115